THE LIGHT GATHERERS

The Light Gatherers

ISBN: 978-1-7371714-9-2 (paperback)
978-1-7376097-0-4 (ebook)

Printed in the United States of America

THE LIGHT GATHERERS

A BOOK WITHIN A BOOK

MICHELLE GARVEY

DEDICATION

For my Moon and Stars

Always shine your brightest

PROLOGUE

"Prime Minister, they're here."

"All of them?"

"Yes, all seven."

"Seven?" He said there would be eight.

"Yes, seven."

"Okay, seven, well ... Thank you, please show them in."

"Seven? Six gatherers, one guardian ,and one keeper, that's eight," she whispered to herself. "Is it strange that I'm nervous? I'm shaking. Why am I shaking? Why am I nervous, and more importantly, why am I talking to myself?"

She could hear footsteps walking closer to her office door. She could picture them walking along the corridor, along the gray well-trodden carpet that many others had walked before them; none perhaps as important as them. Her heart was pounding faster and faster. She stood nervously behind her desk, flanked with the national flag on either side. She quickly scanned the room, making sure everything was in its place. And then the door opened and in walked the six light gatherers and one other.

PART ONE

KAURI POINT VILLAGE

NEW ZEALAND

2022

CHAPTER ONE

She wept as the soldier ripped her child from her arms. Her feet rooted to the ground, unable to move. The deafening thumping and pounding of the surrounding army drowned out the child's screams. The mother could only look on in horror. Frozen with fear and disbelief as her child was flung into—

"Oh my god, can life be any more boring?"

Kat peered above the tattered ancient book that she was reading and saw, standing in front of her, a tallish boy of slim build and short dark brownish hair that had far too much product in it for her liking. He was a handsome boy by all accounts, although Kat would never tell him that. Everyone else seemed to do that for her. And boy, did he use that to his advantage to get whatever he wanted. This usually meant pies—yes, pies. The more the better. Dressed in jeans and a blue T-shirt, she watched as he anxiously shifted from one foot to the other. Hands on his hips with a look of complete bewilderment. Disbelief stretched across his face.

"How can we"—he said, pointing to himself and Kat—"come from those two?" He pointed in the general direction of the two figures sitting at the dining table who were completely oblivious that Kat and Aramis were even in the same room.

Aramis and Kat Praelia were almost fourteen-year-old twins. Aramis was a typical sport- and music-loving boy and Kat was a not-so-typical fourteen-year-old book-loving girl. To them, their quiet life in a small seaside village was the bane of their existence, but all of that was about to change.

"Um, helloooooo, I'm reading here," Kat snapped, frowning at her brother.

"Technically, you're not reading because you're speaking to me" Aramis said with a huff, "But, seriously how on earth can they be our parents? Look at them," he rolled his eyes in complete disbelief.

"What's this rubbish?" he said, turning his full attention to Kat and her book.

"Just because this doesn't come with a remote does not mean it's rubbish," she replied defensively. Kat tried to get back to her book, but she could feel her brother glaring at her. "What?" she grunted at her brother.

"Look at you!" he hissed back. "Day by day, you're turning into them. Next thing you'll be telling me to feel the book and see if it talks to me, become one with the book. What are you now, a friggin' book whisperer?" Aramis said with a look of complete disgust on his face and a touch of disappointment that his twin could be turning out to be just like their parents.

"Oh, what complete rubbish," Kat said, leaning back in her chair. *But he does have a point*, she thought looking at her parents. "What ... what do you want? I'm trying to read about the star of peace."

"Don't tell me you actually paid money for that old book!" Aramis said, huffing again. Kat could almost hear his eyes rolling to the back of his head.

"No, actually ... I found it in Lu's office." Kat replied with a tone that let her brother know just how bored she was getting of this conversation. "It was holding open the door, inside a beautifully carved old box. It's about an angel who makes a star from his soul and gives it to mankind, but they misuse it and ..."

"Yup, okay, interesting," Aramis answered sarcastically.

"Well, you did ask," Kat mumbled, peering down at the old pages.

Aramis sighed. "Come on, Kat. Put the damn book down and come and play this new game I downloaded," Aramis demanded, stamping his feet.

Kat was busy trying to drown out his incessant moaning with the beautifully worded book. "How old do you think it is?" she whispered, running her hand across the page. She felt as if she should have been wearing white gloves.

"Who cares about that old stuff? Come on," Aramis scoffed, becoming more and more impatient.

Kat sat, still staring at the book, refusing to budge. "How old do you think it is though?" she asked Aramis this time. "I dunno," he grunted. "Really old..."

Finally giving up, Aramis threw himself onto the sofa, grunting as if he was in severe pain. "What's it about then?" he asked with a sigh - pretending to be vaguely interested.

"It's in Greek or maybe Latin. I'm not sure but I think it's about an angel who made a star from their heart in the hope that it would guide mankind to love or peace or maybe ... both. It says that the great flood, the sinking of Atlantis, Pompeii being buried, and other catastrophes were all due to the star being held by the wrong people. There are some pages missing and someone has scribbled notes in the margain" She felt like a treasure hunter on the cusp of a great adventure. She could feel the history absorb through her fingers as she leafed through the tattered pages. The book didn't just seem old like the books her parents had. It seemed ancient.

Aramis, who had the attention span of a sand fly, spurted out, "Oh my god, even my eyes are yawning. An angel, seriously? Like one of those little fat kids that fly around with a bow and arrow, someone wrote about them?" he moaned as if he were constipated. "Let's go down to the shops. Lu is talking to some dude out the back. I think he's asking her out," he said with a scoff.

"Those fat kids are called cherubs," Kat said with a huff at her brother "and no, it's not about them," She put the book back in the box. "But I'm going to read that book when we get back. It seems familiar."

Aramis rolled his eyes at her, "It looks like one of those mankey old books that our parents spend all their time going over."

Their parents sat opposite them and were surrounded by piles upon piles of books so high that the twins could barely see them. They weren't interesting books. They were really old religious manuscript-type books. Their parents always seemed to be searching through the books for something, some secret passage in the old mysterious books. They loved them. The mustier those books were the better, as far as their parents were concerned.

"We better go next door and let Lu know where we're going. Go tell her and I'll pack up here," said Kat as she motioned Aramis out the door.

"Okay, then but don't be too long," Aramis whined, glaring at Kat. Their parents didn't even look up as Aramis left.

Ashleigh and Luke Praelia - their wildly dull, book-loving parents were professors at the local university and hardly ever noticed when the twins were in the room. They were so involved with themselves, each other and their work that the twins didn't seem to exist at all.

If it wasn't for their aunt Lu, as the twins called her, the twins probably could have died of starvation and neglect. Not to be dramatic, but they would have probably died. Their parents just didn't seem to care.

The twins spent almost every moment of their time at their Aunt Lu's who lived next door. No one was sure when Lu came into their lives, or how exactly she was related to the twins. All they knew was that she must be related because Kat was a spitting image of her. Lu was fun and caring and is the complete opposite to the twins' parents.

Lu was tall and slim with deep auburn tresses of hair that fell around her shoulders and big sparkling hazel eyes. She had an olive complexion and a scattering of perfectly placed freckles across her face. They seemed to give her an luminous look, and as she walked. She exuded confidence that drew everyone immediately to her.

The twins' mother Ashleigh loved plaid. Brown plain. Brown on brown with more brown. She wore brown flat lace-up shoes, with sagging long brown socks and longish brown and beige plaid skirts nearly down to her ankles. All topped off with a long brown cardi. Sometimes she liked to wear tweed. Brown tweed. Her thick brown-rimmed glasses balanced on her beige freckled face, with her big thick brown bushy eyebrows and her brown frizzy wild hair that was hardly ever brushed. It resembled more of a bird's nest than hair. She always looked like a round brown ball with a bird's nest on top that had recently received an electric shock.

The twins' father, Luke, was the male version of their mother. Except he preferred the colour green. Forest green being his favourite. He wore forest green corduroy trousers with a green cardi and a light green shirt. Topped with green lace-up leather shoes and thick, green-rimmed round glasses. Together they looked like a tree - brown and green. His shortish hair barely covered his large head and was compensated by his enormous unkept beard. His beard was so unruly and frizzy that it too could have been mistaken for a bird's nest. You wouldn't be surprised if an actual bird were living in it.

Ashleigh and Luke Praelia were so out of touch with reality that it seemed kinder to leave them in their happy place of books, pots of decaffeinated Himalayan green tea and vegan fruit cake. They could have been hippies, cool hippies if they were a little edgier. But instead they were dowdy, frumpy, fumbling, boring bike-riding vegan professors with fogged-up jam jar glasses who were more engrossed in their work than anything else.

Their parents were boring.

But Lu wasn't. She laughed and joked and played with the twins. She taught them several different languages including French, Spanish, and Arabic. She had tattoos on her wrists and had travelled a lot. She had even been married once. To the love of her life she said. The twins didn't know what had really happened to him and whenever they asked Lu would just say "He is lost in time". Her eyes would sparkle when she would talk about him and she still wore her wedding ring, a gold band of flowers. Around her neck she wore a pale opalescent blue crystal necklace that seemed to glow. She said that it was given to her by her mother and her mother before. And when she married, she gave half of the crystal to her husband and she wore the other half, symbolizing their union.

If Lu was a rainbow their parents were a boring black and white film.

Their parents' house was dark and dimly lit. It was gloomy. The heavy brown moth-eaten curtains covered every window and always seemed to remain closed. It looked like a set from a Victorian-style horror movie. A reddish, muted brown carpet ran throughout the house. It smelt and looked like a wet, matted dog.

Lu loved colour— all colours—and the brighter, the better. She lived in a house that always seemed to be bright even on a cold gray day. It was always filled with flowers, and the whitewashed walls and white washed wooden floors played host to a menagerie of colours. A crystal chandelier in the hall glistened in the sunlight throwing an assortment of rainbows that danced happily across the walls from room to room. Lu's house had a white picket fence and the front yard was filled with flowers. The twins felt safe there.

CHAPTER TWO

Aramis sighed as he pushed open the gate to Lu's house. The breeze stirring up all the different scents in Lu's garden. Suddenly, as quick as the flick of a switch, he felt nauseous and queasy. He could feel a headache coming on as he keeled over in pain. He had never felt like this before. He was woozy, short of breath, panicked. There was a buzzing noise in his ears and his eyes blurred over like Vaseline on glass. Lu and the man both turned and looked startled. As if Aramis had interrupted something very important. *He looked vaguely familiar,* Aramis thought as he stumbled - almost losing his balance.

"I better be off, but you need to be careful. We can't protect you." The man quietly said to Lu.

Aramis had never felt as awkward as he did just at that moment. He could barely see the outline of Lu putting her hand up to the man's face and kissing him on the cheek. She then whispered something to him and hugged him. As he walked past, he pulled his cap right down. Aramis couldn't see his face very well, but he did notice that the man had the same blue crystal as Lu, only smaller.

"Oh, darling, are you okay?" Lu asked, motioning Aramis to sit down on the garden bench.

"Yeah, I am. I just felt sick. It came on really fast. I don't know what happened. Who was that? Was that your husband?"

"Who was who, darling?" Lu said, she pressed the back of her hand to his forehead "How do you feel now?" The air brushed up against his face gently cooling him

"I'm actually okay now, which is weird, but who was that guy? He had a crystal like yours. Is he related?" Aramis asked curiously.

"Maybe it was something you ate or maybe it was actually coming outside into the fresh air," Lu teased, looking at Aramis.

"Maybe," he mumbled, trying to figure out what made him feel that way.

"Did you come out to tell me something or did you come to help me in the garden?"

"Oh yeah, Kat and I were just going down to the shops. Would you like us to get you anything?"

"No, thanks, have a good time and be home before dinner, I'm making your favorite," she said.

"Noodles? Are we having spicy noodles with cashews for dinner?"

"Yep," Lu said, nodding her head as she walked back into the house. Aramis noticed she looked a little worried after the man left. There was just something familiar about him. Aramis couldn't put his finger on it.

Walking toward the shops, Aramis was still trying to figure out what had made him feel so sick and then how he recovered so fast, and then he wondered who that man was. "Lu never did tell me who he was," Aramis said to Kat nearing the shop.

Just then the twins noticed their parents in their car, an old station wagon that they had nicknamed "Old Bess" moving slowly down the road. The twins' parents would go to conferences out of town every two weeks but they only went away last weekend.

"Nice of them to tell us that they were going away. I swear to God, sometimes I think that they just forget that we are even here," Kat said, disappointingly looking toward the car driving out of the village. She was always making excuses for her parents' detachment and indifference to them. She turned to go into the shop and then realized that she had left her purse in the car.

"Blast!" she said. "I need my purse."

"Whhhaaatttttt!" Aramis groaned.

"If you want a pie, we're gonna have to catch up to Mum and Dad," Kat said in her bossy little voice.

"Maybe we can catch up to them at the bridge if we cut through Deadman's Field," Aramis said almost defiantly.

Deadman's Field. The thought of it made Kat shudder. Deadman's Field ran alongside the river, separating the river from the town. It was mostly flat and littered with dead willow trees that refused to fall down. Even in the middle of summer the field felt cold. Hundreds of years ago a man was found dead in the field. Dressed in strange clothing for the area and time. It left the field with a strange eerie feeling. Nothing grew there anymore, not even weeds. And no one went through the field either.

Kat looked at the field, and then back at her parents winding their way out of the village center.

"Okay, let's do it," she said with an air of regret in her voice.

And with that, they sprinted down the road and across the open fields. As they ran, Kat felt as if someone or something was trying to grab her. She sprinted to the bridge with all of her heart. The fastest that she had ever run. Even Aramis was having a little trouble keeping up with her.

The bridge was right there. Just in sight. But where were their parents? Out of breath the twins scrambled up on the bridge and out of the field's grasp

"What the hell was that?" Aramis said, doubled over trying to catch his breath. "I've never seen you run so fast."

Kat had her arms up with her hands behind her head also trying to catch her breath.

"Couldn't you feel them?" she said, gasping for air.

"Who?" Aramis replied puzzled

"In the field, I could feel them trying to grab me, around my feet and legs," she said, pacing. "I am never going back through that field again."

"You do realize that if there was something in the field they could get up here too," he mocked.

"Stop it. You're scaring me. Where is Mum and Dad?" Kat mumbled as she looked up and down the gravel road searching for them.

"Where the hell are they?" said Aramis, frowning.

As they rounded the corner, they just caught a glimpse of the back of their parents' station wagon pulling into an old garage on the edge of the village. The garage was all that was left of a big old house that was destroyed by fire years ago.

"What are they doing? Why are they in the garage?" Kat asked

The twins started running over yelling out to their parents. They reach the garage and burst through the doors. But their parents weren't there. Only their old station wagon car.

"That's not possible, "Kat said, puzzled. "We just saw them drive in. We just saw Dad close the garage door so where are they?" They looked under the car and all around but their parents weren't there.

Aramis put his hand on the bonnet. It was still hot from being driven. But where could they have gone? There was only one way in and out and the twins were at the door, so they didn't leave that way.

"They're not in the car and there aren't any side or back doors. We're not going mad. They actually were here, weren't they?" Kat asked Aramis for reassurance

"Yep, that's our car, and it's still warm" Aramis shrugged

Kat grabbed her purse out of the car and said, "Let's get outta here. This place is creeping me out."

The twins ran back to Lu's place and told her what had happened. Interestingly Lu didn't look as shocked as they thought she would have been.

"They must've gone out the side door, "she said to them in a dismissive voice.

"Side door, there's no side door, it's all stone". Aramis spurted out, throwing himself down onto the sofa as if he had just completed a marathon. Nothing was adding up. This whole day had been off.

"Well, they couldn't have disappeared into thin air. I was talking to your mother, she said that they have had to go on an emergency trip for a few days but will be back on Monday, so you're spending the weekend with me."

"Not like that's anything new," Aramis muttered under his breath while looking for the TV remote. Kat looked worried.

"Don't worry, Kat. Your parents will be fine. People can't just vanish, can they?" Lu said, turning back to do the dishes.

Kat wasn't so much worried about her parents as curious as to how they weren't in the garage. Both Kat and Aramis had played in that garage millions of times when they were younger and there were absolutely no side doors. Just side walls and a rolling door with a floor of rock but definitely no side door, no back door. Nothing.

Kat walked into the study and sat down pulling out the carved box. She pulled out the old tattered book hoping it would take her mind off her parents. She had a nagging feeling that this book had something to do with them. She just didn't know how. And what was that torn page about? The ink was barely visible. Why would someone rip half of it? Where's the other part and why is that important?

CHAPTER THREE

Kat decided to research the book and box. She couldn't believe all of the information she was finding. Website after website talked about ancient civilizations across the world that all told of a star of peace and for centuries armies had gone to war in the hope of owning it. All wars throughout history were searching for the ultimate holy relic. A relic that would grant the owner success in whatever they desired. A relic that held such power to allow the owner to conquer all of mankind if they so wished.

Kat briefly imagined herself in an Indiana Jones hat and satchel in some far-off land, surrounded by desert looking off into the distance searching for that very elusive relic.

A few websites even mentioned a prophecy that was reportedly thousands of years old. That roughly translated to "the pieces of the star will be reunited by 11 of Adam and Eve and joined by one who is of humanity".

All around the world, ancient civilizations all had variations of the old prophecy, that the star be reformed by 11 and held by 1.

It's a modern day treasure hunt.

She was so engrossed in her self made mission of discovery that she lost track of the time.

Website after website all mentioned a book made of vellum with a Merkaba and constellations on the cover. Just like the book she had! They talked about a map that is dead until light from the star shines and then the map is revealed, illuminating locations of the remaining pieces of the star. The light from the star opens history to the holder.

Apparently, from what Kat could make out from the scribbles in pencil on the book and the websites each piece opens a certain doorway into the past. *But how can that be?* she thought and surely it's not physical doorways, that's just impossible.

"ARAMIS!" Kat screamed, "COME HERE NOWWWWWWWWWWWWW!" she commanded. "Oh my goodness, I can't believe it," Kat said to herself, clutching the book and her laptop as she ran out of the study to grab Aramis.

"What, what's wrong?" Aramis said, jumping up, half expecting Kat to be incapacitated

"You've gotta read this. Come on," Kat insisted

"WOAH, are you serious? You screamed for me to come to you for that grotty old book?"

He stood, glaring at Kat with his hands on his hips in disbelief.

"I found out all of this stuff and I think that it's Lu's book." She waved the book up to Aramis' face. He swiped it away in disgust.

"There is only one that was ever written and the holder of it is some great magical priest or priestess that knows the exact location of each of the pieces. The priest or priestess can see through time" Aramis rolled his eyes "And that person leads and guides the guardians and the gatherers. The identity of the priest or priestess is never known. It's always a secret," she said excitedly.

"And you think Lu is the priestess?" Aramis mocked, "Think about this. Have you ever seen Lu even read a book? She's the complete opposite to Mum and Dad."

Kat laughed and nodded her head, "Yep. You're right. Lu would never be the priestess" Kat was disappointed. But then quickly came up with another theory. "But what if it was left in the house and it's the lost book of peace? Do you know that there was a group or organization called the Enlightened or the Circle of Light, or is it the

Council of Light?" Kat said while flicking through her pages on her laptop thoroughly determined to find the exact passage

"Yeah, I've heard of them. They were a secret sect that travelled through time, gathering pieces of the star to rule the world," Aramis said.

"Exactly, wow, so you've heard of them?" Kat said excitedly and slightly surprised. "So you know that this must be the Book of Peace, right?"

"No, Kat, of course I haven't bloody well heard of them. I haven't heard of them because they don't blimmen well exist! Seriously, Kat? You must be kidding," Aramis said with his head in his hands. "You pulled me away from my game for this rubbish?" he said sarcastically.

"Oh, be quiet, I dunno," Kat said. "This feels real."

"Feels? What are you talking about? Geez, why do you believe in everything, Kat?" Aramis sighed, throwing his hands in the air at the thought of his sister being so gullible.

"What if, just imagine for one minute that it is real. That there really is a book of peace and an angel really did create a star from their soul. The angel hid pieces of the star throughout time around the world, and the pieces of the star act as keys to different dimensions or times. I don't know. It's just a theory, but it feels right," she said, staring at the book.

Aramis sat, not quite believing what was coming out of his sister's mouth.

Then he said, "Okay, so let's just say that it is true," with a factual tone in his voice.

"One, how can you travel through time? You can't. It's impossible. If it was possible, you would have all of those nutters going back and erasing mankind, soooo no. Two, if an angel existed, why hasn't anyone seen one? I mean really seen one. Like walking down the road with their big wings dragging along the ground. Soooo yeah, nah."

"I'm gonna investigate it further. This website here said that a Templar had one piece of the star. That it was from his wife who died in a fire along with his small children. Awww, that's so sad," Kat said, her eyes welling up while reading about the Templar's family.

Aramis sighed "Whoever wrote that needs to do their homework first. Templars weren't allowed to have any personal belongings so whoever wrote that story is wrong! And secondly, a Templar doesn't marry and have families," Aramis said, sitting down on the sofa, looking bored.

"But what if a Templar did have the piece? What if all of this was true? You see this sun on the front of the box" she shoved the box on to Aramis' lap "I've found reference to it and it refers to the brotherhood or sisterhood of light and the constellations arranged in that order I think is for the circle of the enlightened. Both secret religious organizations."

"Yep cool story, mate. They're so secret that no one has ever heard of them," Aramis mumbled, pushing the box away.

But Kat couldn't stop.

"Both were set up to collect and protect the pieces of the star, but apparently, there are something like thirteen pieces and they have found one. And you would be able to tell if you had a piece of the star just by holding it over the map, which by the way looks vaguely similar to the ripped page in the book." Kat had an exciting tone to her voice that would compel anyone to follow her, anyone except her twin Aramis.

"Are you talking to me?" Aramis asked. "Or are you just thinking out loud? Lu has crystals everywhere. Why don't you go and see if any of those do anything and I will go back to my game," he grunted putting his headphones back on.

Excited, Kat gathered all of the crystals in the house and one by one put them on the ripped page in the book, and to her dismay, nothing, absolutely nothing, happened.

"What are you two up to?" a voice said.

The twins both looked up to see Lu standing over them.

"Kat thinks you're a magical priestess and your manky old book is the world-famous Book of Peace," Aramis said, strutting out of the room with his mouth half full.

"What, a priestess, me? Well, thank you. But I prefer the term goddess," Lu said, smiling at Kat. "What's all this about, a book of peace?" Lu asked

"Well, I did a little bit of research and I found a book that looks like yours..."

"That old thing, I bought it at a garage sale for five cents. I thought it made a great door stop," Lu said, interrupting Kat.

Kat looked slightly disappointed.

"So, tell me what you found out," Lu sat, listening to Kat tell all about the magical powers of the priestess and the book, the king of kings, and the king of sands, how armies have searched for the book and the priest or priestess over time.

For the next few days, Kat was obsessed, searching for every little bit of information she could find. She was convinced that Lu's book was the ancient Book of Peace and that it would lead to the Star of Peace.

What Kat didn't know was that she was on the right path, a dangerous and important path, that would not only change her and Aramis's life but would change the lives of all of those around her.

CHAPTER FOUR

"Kids, your father and I have to go out of town again this weekend and Lu will be looking after you," Ashleigh rattled off the news, oblivious to Kat's feelings.

Kat was frowning. "This weekend, Mum? Do you really have to go?"

"Yes, Kat" Ashleigh said, turning her attention back to one of the musty books "your father and I have an important conference." That was it. End of discussion.

"But..." Kat looked down, her eyes filled with tears. Aramis nudged her toward the door and said, "Let's go outside, mate."

They walked into the cool breeze. Aramis first, followed by a very sad Kat.

"What's up with the sad face? They always go away. How is this any different?"

"It's the eighth of November today, and Saturday will be the eleventh of November" recognition dawned on Aramis' face. Kat continued on "We will be fourteen! And for once, just once, I thought that they would remember,"

Kat looked like a wilted, droopy flower

"Come on. Let's go over to Lu's and you can continue your research into the star of Pete," he said, nudging his sister.

"It's called the star of peace," she huffed

"Hahahaha! Yeah, that would make more sense," Aramis joked. Suddenly he grabbed Kat - pulling her to a stop. She looked at him, fed up.

"I have an idea. What if we followed the hippies" (the hippies being their parents) "on Saturday? We could hide in the garage and see exactly how they get out,"

"Where on earth are we gonna hide?" Kat snarled. "There's nothing in the garage. It's empty."

"Well," he was thinking so much she could almost see smoke coming out of his ears, "we'll just have to improvise."

Saturday rolled around quicker than Kat had run across Deadman's Field. Along with it, the smell of freshly cooked waffles wafted through the air. Christmas carols played in the background even though it wasn't Christmas. It could only ever mean one thing, the twins were at Lu's place.

Every morning started the same way, with Lu standing in the hallway singing "Good morning, my shining stars." It was kind of nice and the twins loved every minute of waking up there.

Walking into the kitchen, the twins saw a huge banner strung across the entire width of the breakfast area. H A P P Y B I R T H D A Y was written in large, bright letters.

"Happy birthday, my darlings. You're fourteen today and I have big plans for us all."

"We have big plans as well," Aramis whispered under his breath while trying to stuff four waffles in his mouth all at once.

"Hurry up and have breakfast so you can go and say goodbye to your parents, but don't be too hard on them if they don't remember that it's your birthday. You know what they're like."

"Okay, we will." Aramis kissed Lu on her cheek. Just then he noticed that she wasn't wearing her blue crystal around her neck.

"But open your present from me before you go."

Kat picked up a beautifully wrapped gift; blush-coloured paper with a giant bow. She tugged at the ribbon letting the paper fall aside to reveal a light blue opalescent crystal that resembled a portion of Lu's crystal. The one that she always wore. Kats' eyes filled with tears as she looked up at Lu.

"I love you with all my heart," she whispered. Tears rolled down Kat's cheek as Lu placed the necklace around her neck.

"But it's your necklace," Kat said, choking on her tears.

"It's part of my necklace."

Aramis opened his gift wrapped in pale blue paper. It was the same as Kat's, part of Lu's necklace. She put it around Aramis's neck and lightly kissed him on the cheek as well.

She whispered, "I know it's not very blokey for rugby players to wear necklaces but..."

"I love it," Aramis said.

"You two mean the world to me, more than you will ever know," Lu said, hugging the twins. Although Aramis almost never cried or showed any hint of emotion, Kat could have sworn that she saw his eyes well with tears.

"Now all the people that I love have part of my heart, my necklace. You see, I still have a bit. You two have a bit and my husband has half." *Has?* Aramis thought to himself. Lu didn't say *had*. She said has. So he's still alive? Maybe he was the man in the back garden. Aramis stood there puzzled lost in his thoughts.

"Okay, okay, go and say goodbye to your parents. Hurry up before you miss them." Lu gave both of them a huge hug and they ran out to say goodbye to their parents.

In their own way, their parents did love the twins. Kat was sure of that but they just showed it differently to Lu. They were always quite cold and distant toward the twins.

Aramis and Kat both said goodbye and said that they had to run errands for Lu. As predicted, their parents made absolutely no mention of their birthday. The twins ran into their garage and quickly climbed into the back of their parents' station wagon, hiding under the old blankets.

The next thing they knew, their parents were in the car. They didn't even put bags or suitcases in, which both Aramis and Kat thought was weird.

The car started and Kat and Aramis listened to their parents talking. They heard Ashleigh ask Luke what the date was. Luke said the eleventh of November, and they both listened, waiting for some resemblance of their parents remembering their birthday. They were both disappointed as neither of them mentioned anything about them or their birthday. They mentioned numbers and dates and Ashleigh seemed to be reading coordinates, which made no sense at all. Then the car started slowing down and they knew that they were pulling into the driveway of the old burnt down house. They heard their dad's car door open and then they could hear the garage door open. Luke got back into the car and drove in. Ashleigh got out of the car and they heard the rattling of the garage door closing at the same time Luke got out.

Both Kat and Aramis peered out the car window watching their parents. Kat still had tears rolling down her cheek.

"Don't worry," Aramis said, "You know how those two forget everything," he said, nudging her. "They're bloody useless, you know that," he said, smiling.

But Kat wasn't smiling. "What the hell is that? she whispered.

Aramis' jaw dropped. "Bloody hell, what is it?"

Right in front of them, they saw as clear as day their mother draw on the side of the garage the shape of a door. The door opened. The twins could see right through the opening—a tunnel of swirling lights, clouds, and stars, but at the end, right at the very end, they could see people walking past, just going about their merry way as if there was nothing out of the ordinary. They watched as their parents walked through.

Kat noticed that her mother's hair looked like she had brushed it and she wasn't actually wearing brown plaid. In fact, from behind, she looked completely different.

Then the opening - that magical door - started closing.

"Nooooooo!" Aramis exclaimed with despair and panic racing through his entire body. He jumped up, throwing off the blankets. He scrambled over the seats and was out the car door faster than Kat had ever seen him move before. By the time she got out of the car, Aramis was touching the wall where he had just seen his parents disappear through.

"This can't be ... scientifically our parents couldn't just walk through a garage wall," he said, looking at the blank wall of rock.

"Aramis," Kat's voice sounded scared. "Aramis," she said again.

"What?" he answered, still looking at the wall in disbelief.

"ARAMIS!" she said again, hitting his arm.

"What!" He turned to look at her. "Oh my god, Kat, look at your necklace."

"Look at yours," she said.

The twins' necklaces were levitating like magnets towards the wall. "I saw Mum use something to draw an outline of a door. What if I use my necklace to draw a door? That might work," she mumbled.

Encouragingly Aramis said, "Go on then see what happens."

Kat slowly started to draw an outline of a door using the crystal on her necklace. As she started drawing she noticed her necklace glowed a bright strong blue, almost neon in colour.

Kat stopped and lifted the crystal off the wall. The outline quickly disappeared and the crystal stopped glowing. She pressed the crystal back to the wall and the outline reappeared. Her hand trembling with a mix of fear and excitement she continued to complete the outline of the door. Then within a second the wall seemed to completely dissolve and a tunnel of bright lights and stars swirling around in a haze of fog appeared. And at the end, the twins could see people walking by, not even noticing the swirl of fog that resembled the inside of a tornado on its side that had swept up thousands of stars and planets swished together with a thick layer of fog.

The twins took a deep breath and looked at each other.

"Are we doing this?" Kat said.

"It'll be rude not to," Aramis said, breathing hard and looking forward.

They looked at each other with wild eyes. Then both stepped forward, and with that, they seemed to be on a speeding conveyor belt. The ground was moving and they felt like they were being sucked towards the end. Like a giant magnet was pulling them towards the opening. The deafening noise of what seemed like a thousand drums beating at all different speeds and intensities coupled with bright lights flashing past the twins microseconds at a time completely disorientated them.

Both felt as if they were inside a giant washing machine without the water spinning round and around and around until they could barely breathe.

The flashing and swirling lights, the clashing deafening sounds, and the feeling of the ground moving beneath them was overwhelming. Both Aramis and Kat were screaming and lost their balance when what seemed like hours of the stomach-churning hazy fog stopped and they were lying on a cobbled street.

PART TWO

FRANCE

1944

CHAPTER FIVE

"Where are we?" Aramis said, his throat was dry from all the screaming in the tunnel. Nothing seemed to make any sense at all. Disorientated and feeling physically ill, Kat dragged herself to the closest wall and leant up against it. Her heart was beating so fast and so loud she was sure that everyone could hear it.

"Where are we?" Aramis repeated, looking around. "And why is everything written in French? Whoa, what just happened?" he said, startled, the signs now suddenly in English "I just saw the shop signs literally change from French to English right in front of my eyes." He turned to look at Kat and noticed she was sitting on the ground up against the wall, with her knees up against her chest. She was a pasty white colour and looked like she was about to vomit.

"Kat," he said, running over to her. "Are you okay?" he asked.

Kat had her head buried in her hands. "I don't feel good. I really don't," she said in a slow, woozy voice. "I'm not good," she said, looking up at Aramis. He looked worried. That was the first time she had ever seen him look worried. He always put a sarcastic spin on everything that always made her laugh but this time he was frowning and staring so intensely at her that it gave her goosebumps.

"What do you need?" he asked Kat.

"Just give me a few minutes," she said. "I'll be fine."

He sat down beside and she rested her head on his shoulder.

"I never stop to think about what I put you through. I always just think about how much fun it will be but I think we should just go back home," he said, hugging her.

"Whhhaaaatttt? You must be kidding. I didn't just go through that damn tunnel to turn around and go back home. No way, Jose. We are going to find our parents and find out what the hell is going on," Kat said rather assertively, and with that, she stood up, brushed off her clothes, and started to gather her bearings.

Aramis jumped up, grinning. "That's my little sis, and by little I mean in height, not age," he said.

"Easy on the little. I was born before you," she snarled.

"But I'm taller," he joked back.

"Hmmmmm, where are we, and why is everything written in French?" she asked.

"Wait, you can see everything in French. When we first came out of the tunnel, I saw French and then it all changed to English right in front of me," Aramis said in disbelief. "But if I can see it in English. How come you can't?"

"I dunno," Kat said puzzled. "Maybe because I'm not feeling the best?"

"Maybe, but one thing's for sure, we can't stand around here all day, and I have no idea where to start searching for the hippies."

Kat smiled as Aramis started to get his humor back.

"Well, obviously, we are in a French-speaking country."

"Or a film set," Aramis butted in. "I'm leaning towards a film set," he said, looking around and nodding.

"I think we're in a French-speaking country," Kat said, smiling at her brother.

"Maybe the crystals translate everything so we can understand them," she said. She went to reach for her crystal but only felt an empty space around her neck. "It's gone. Where is it?" she gasped, panicking, looking around.

Aramis scanned the floor and spotted it near where the tunnel had spat them out. "Here ... here it is." he picked it up and handed it to Kat.

"Thank goodness, I better get this chain fixed," she murmured. As she held the crystal, she instantly started to feel better and then she noticed that all the signs turned from French to English.

"That's amazing," she said in awe. "I can understand everything."

As people walked past, they could understand their conversations. They could read the signs and newspapers. The twins then realized that the crystals not only protected but also acted as some sort of translator.

They saw people in military uniforms and the date on the newspaper said 1944.

"1944," Kat said, thinking of what she had learnt at school. "What do we know?" she asked Aramis as they looked at the paper.

Aramis looked at her flabbergasted "We cannot be in 1944. That's impossible, 1944 France? No, it's a film set," he said.

CHAPTER SIX

"We are in a French-speaking town and people are wearing German uniforms" trying to work it all out in her head "Oh my god, are we in France in World War 2?" she said. "We can't be. That would mean that we have gone back in time" she cried, answering her own question. "A war? Why would our parents be here? In a war of all places. And how can we find them?" Her voice started to get higher and higher the more distressed she became.

As they walked around the town, Aramis became more and more convinced that it was a film set for Beauty and the Beast and half expected to see Belle walking down the road singing "Bonjour."

They sat down trying to figure out what their next step was when they noticed people gathering opposite them, all staring and pointing at them. There must've been at least nine or ten of them.

"Aramis," Kat said in a hasty, worried voice, looking at Aramis.

"Yep," he answered. "I'm hungry." He was looking toward a bread shop. "I wonder if they sell pies."

"I think we have bigger problems other than your stomach," Kat said.

As he looked up, the group that was gathered opposite them were now standing in front of them.

"Who are you?" one of them asked. "Where are your papers? Show me them."

"What are those?" another said, pointing at Aramis's feet.

"Ummm, they would be shoes." He was about to lunge into a sarcastic rant when Kat stopped him with a stare, letting him know that now was not the best time to do that.

"Oh, papers ummm, sure, I'll just have a look in my bag," she said, trying to stall for time until she came up with an idea. "You know it's a pity that you have to be so rude to us because..."

One of them interrupted, saying, "They're spies. They know. Look at their clothes. Take them now before they're noticed." In a scared voice, he added, "Hurry."

"Take us, take us where?" Kat cried. "What do we know? We don't know anything. Please we're looking for our parents, Ashleigh and Luke. Maybe you've heard of them? Please ... we're only fourteen. We know nothing."

"Get off me," Aramis said as two men dragged him from the street.

"Quiet," one of them whispered. "You do not want the Germans to come over, do you?" He grunted, smelling heavily of tobacco.

The group dispersed and Aramis and Kat were taken to what could've been an abandoned store and were thrown down some stairs into a dark damp basement. The door slammed behind them and they heard a key turn in the lock.

"I'm scared," Kat said, holding onto Aramis.

"It'll be okay. We'll get out of here. I just need to figure out how."

They heard shuffling and people above them. They could hear what sounded like furniture being dragged across the floor, which seemed to stop in front of what sounded like the door they had been thrown through. Their hearts sank. In the dark they could barely see each other. Hours seemed to pass and they heard muffled voices and doors slam. They heard people come and go. They heard someone running across the floorboards above them. They smelt food cooking and laughter. They thought that someone must've known their parents why they weren't handed over to the Germans, but their parents never came.

The twins lost all sense of time and wondered if they were ever going to survive. Aramis knew that Kat was terrified of the dark and as they sat on the damp earth floor of the basement he started to make up stories in the hope of making his sister smile. He couldn't bear the thought of her being scared.

He started telling her a story of a brother and sister. The brother was tall and handsome while the sister was as tiny as the tiniest mouse. He could feel Kat listening and he knew that she was smiling.

"Mouse," she said. "This is France in 1944. The white mouse is here, somewhere here in France," she said in an excited voice.

"Oh yeah, that Kiwi chick that was the gestapo's most wanted. She was pretty cool aye," Aramis said, knowing that she was one of Kat's idols.

"She was," Kat said, "or should I say *is*, because she's still alive in 1944!!" Kat seemed to cheer up a bit.

"I wonder what those people meant when they said we know and look at their clothes. I'm pretty sure they had jeans in 1944," Aramis said aloud, trying to recall anything from school. *Nah, I'm drawing a blank* he thought to himself as he tried to recall any glimmer of anything from his boring classes.

The basement started to get colder and colder and the twins huddled together to keep warm as they struggled to keep their eyes open. Filled with fear, tiredness crept over them like smog over a modern city. *We can't die here*, Kat thought defiantly as she drifted off to sleep. *We can't!*

CHAPTER SEVEN

"Kat! Kat! What are you doing here?" a woman's voice whispered. It was an unknown voice, but at the same time, there seemed to be something vaguely familiar. Kat tried to see who the woman was and where she was. But it was no use. Kat had been blindfolded. *Where is Aramis?* she thought. *I need my brother. Where is he?* Fear filled her whole body. She had something around her mouth that stopped her from speaking.

"They can't be here," the voice said to someone else.

Kat tried to open her eyes. *Where is Aramis?* She wanted to reach for him in the dark.

"Put this on them and take them up the hill. I'll be there soon. Where's A.D.?" the woman asked.

"He hasn't arrived yet. Something went wrong."

"What? What do you mean wrong?"

Kat could sense the woman's stress levels accelerating. A.D? Kat remembered seeing the letters A.D in Lu's book. She assumed it meant Anno Domini and not an actual person. She was no longer in the basement. Her hands were tied behind her back. She felt as if she had been drugged. She was groggy and was trying to stay alert. She thought she was going to be sick.

"Give her some water then take her. I'll speak with her brother."

No, no way are you taking me, Kat tried to scream. *Where is my brother? Please, please, don't hurt him,* she thought.

The woman came over to Kat and whispered, "Stop struggling. Aramis will be with you soon." She stroked Kat's hair and kissed her head. Kat, for whatever reason, stopped struggling and calmed down. This woman, whoever she was, made her feel safe. Then she heard her walk out of the room.

The cloth was taken off from around Kat's mouth.

"Drink this," a male voice said as what Kat assumed was a glass pushed up against her mouth and water flooded in, rushing so fast that she started to choke.

"Do you want this gag back on?" the voice asked.

"No," Kat cried, shaking. The ropes around her wrist we're cutting in and she could feel a thick wet trickle of blood dripping down over her hands.

"Then be quiet. I'm going to put this over your head. Do not say a word or it will be going back on. Do you understand?" he said.

Terrified, Kat nodded.

She wanted to go home. She regretted following her parents. She regretted everything. She wanted to be back with Lu in her warm house with spiced hot chocolate. Kat wondered why the crystal wasn't protecting her or Aramis. Maybe she had misinterpreted the writings in the book. Kat felt her body give way as she fell into a slump on the floor. She could feel the warmth of a fire on her face and warm floorboards under her cheek. She then felt herself being lifted. She couldn't hear much, just a loud whirring noise all around her, just like in the tunnel she came through with her brother. Then coldness, icy coldness. She gasped trying to catch her breath. The freshness of the cold air penetrated the bag over her head. She was then thrown into the back of something. She could feel the hardness and coldness of the metal. She couldn't make out where she was and then there was a loud thud beside her. What was it? She could hear it moving.

Kat was paralyzed with fear.

She was in a vehicle. She heard the engine start as she knew she was about to be taken to her death. She couldn't hold back the tears any longer. Then she heard, "As soon as I get out of these bloody ropes, I'm gonna throw you in the back and see how you like it. Yep, keeping chugging away on those smokes, mate. They'll kill you faster than this friggin war, and where the hell is my sister? If you have so much as touched her, I'll ..." it was the voice of her brother.

"Aramis?"

"Kat, where are you?" Aramis wriggled free of the ropes behind his back and took the bag off his head.

"Awww. Thank god, you're okay," he said, taking the bag off Kat's head. "It's gonna be okay." He took the ropes off from around her blood stained wrists. "It's okay," he said, hugging her. Kat was shaking but relieved that her brother was with her. She wrapped her arms around him and immediately felt safe.

"Did they drug you?" she asked

"Drug? No," he replied. "Did they drug you? That's not right. Are you okay? How do you feel?"

"I'm much better now," she said, holding his arm.

"What did they say to you?" she asked.

"There was a lady. I couldn't see her because I was blindfolded. She asked me how old I was, and then why I was there and I said to find our parents although I'm regretting that now. They're bloody useless and couldn't be here. She laughed. It was weird because I know that laugh from somewhere. Then she said, 'Always the joker' but she did up my hoodie and said not to show anyone this, and she touched the crystal. She said that you are fine and they would take me to you"

"Do you think she was Mum?"

"Ashleigh? You must be kidding. That woman was definitely not Ashleigh, but there is something familiar about her I just don't know what," he said.

"We need to get off this truck. I have no idea where they're taking us and I have no intention of finding out," Aramis said, crawling toward the back of the truck.

He looked at Kat. "Are we doing this?"

"Yep." She nodded back.

"When they slow down, we'll make a jump for it, okay?"

The truck was meandering up a windy road. The twins lifted the corner of the tarpaulin and could see the lights from the village miles below them. The icy cold air stung their eyes like the sting of a wasp. They seemed to be going through a forest and the truck didn't have any lights on.

"They're not German, so who are they?" Aramis said

The road started to level out, and they noticed that the truck was slowing down. The twins realized that they were nearing the top of the hill.

"I think now's as good a time as any," Aramis said to Kat

As the truck slowed down to stop, the twins jumped and ran towards the forest. The snow-covered ground crunched under their feet and they discovered that the picturesque snow wasn't as thick as they originally thought.

They heard the truck stop and then they heard voices, lots of voices. They hid to catch their breath. They knew that they couldn't stay where they were for long. They had to keep moving. It was dark and they thought that they should move back down the hill back to the town where they first arrived, then figure out a way to get back to 2022.

Except, the twins suddenly realized, their footprints in the snow would lead anyone searching for them straight to them.

CHAPTER EIGHT

They both looked at each other. Their crystals were glowing just like they had glowed when they were in the garage at home. Maybe it meant that a way for them to get home was closer than heading back into the town.

"The crystals can lead us home," Aramis said, looking at Kat.

"I completely agree. I'm over this," she said. "I just want to go home to boring old Kauri Point Village"

As the kids were looking at the crystals deciding what to do, they were completely oblivious to anything or anyone around them. The air was freezing cold, and their warm breath hit the icy air and floated up into the night sky like smoke signals, saying, "Hey, you over there, here I am."

Aramis felt something press up against his back. He turned and looked at Kat and knew that someone was behind him.

"Move," the voice said. "I've better things to do than chase you idiots around the forest. Keep going, both of you."

They were joined by another person with a rifle who said, "Why didn't you two just stay in the truck? Now we have to deal with this." They recognized the voices from the two that had loaded them into the truck. The twins were pushed into a dark cave. They were told to keep going.

"But where?" Aramis said. "It's a cave." They could see the back of the cave and it was just rock.

"Keep going I said," the man with the rifle pushed Kat.

"THERE'S NOWHERE TO GO!" she yelled back

He motioned her to move to the left and the twins saw a narrow opening. It was completely invisible when viewed straight on but if you moved a little to the side everything changed. *That's pretty clever,* Aramis thought to himself.

There were faint candles sitting in tiny holes carved deep into the rock of the cave. The twins could see the glow from the candles leading deeper and deeper underground. The coldness seemed to dissolve and a rush of warm air greeted them as the cave seemed to level out.

They passed various tunnels and saw crosses with numerals above them, old crosses like Templar crosses and roman numerals. The tunnels seemed ancient.

Lu would love this, Kat thought. *She loves everything to do with Templars. Oh, Lu, I miss her so much. I wish she was with us. She would keep us safe, and where on earth are Mum and Dad?*

CHAPTER NINE

The twins were scared. They had no idea where they were going, but both of them had a dreadful sense that they were going to die. Die in a cave, in an ancient tunnel, in France, in 1944. Kat had tears streaming down her face.

Although Aramis was five minutes younger than her, he was psychically taller than her and was super protective of his sister. A lioness protects her cubs. He was the same and would do anything to keep her safe.

He was desperate to get them out of this situation. They passed side tunnel after side tunnel, and Aramis's mind was ticking over. *If this is a Templar cave, then the tunnels would always have other exit points*, he thought.

Just then they heard more voices behind them. "Don't turn around, keep going," they were told. They had been walking in the cave for at least fifteen minutes. They passed more and more side tunnels, so many that they almost lost count.

"We have a problem," one voice said.

"We know who the traitor is." Kat and Aramis looked at each other still walking.

"Get ready to run," Aramis said to Kat.

"Who?" one of the men from the truck said.

"It's A.D"

"Never," the other man said in disbelief.

"I know I don't believe it either. Does she know?"

"Who, M.D? No, I don't think so. They've got him and are bringing him in. There must be a mistake. He would never betray us."

The twins slowly walked towards a large glow, and as they rounded the corner they could see people all standing around looking at map boards on the walls of the caves, and tables everywhere. There were weapons and at least thirty or forty people in there. They noticed two ladies standing and talking intensely to each while looking toward another tunnel, and one of the ladies was pleading with the other.

They recognized the voice of the woman from the village. The one who told Aramis to hide his crystal.

"That's her, the one from the village," he said to Kat. Kat still wasn't feeling well and was trying to recover from being drugged. The woman turned and said, "What are they doing here?" to the two men behind.

"They jumped out of the truck and were running back to town," he said.

"God, this is all I need," she said. "Why do you two never listen?" she said, shaking her head and then muttered, "As if I didn't know."

The twins looked at each other as if they were supposed to know the woman. She wasn't their mother. Who was she? She looked like a younger Lu but without the accent. When Lu sometimes spoke she would sound almost Spanish.

All of a sudden, all hell broke loose. Coming from one of the other tunnels a group of people were surrounding one man.

"We have him," one of them said.

Kat turned and looked at Aramis. She knew that voice. Aramis turned his head slowly to see where that voice was coming from. Straight away he saw him. He couldn't believe his eyes. Their father was there, right there holding a rifle and pointing it at someone who was being dragged in by others. Aramis was starting to feel sick like Kat. Maybe they had drugged him after all.

The prisoner was struggling as he was being dragged towards a makeshift room to the side of the tunnel and was being led by at least four other armed men, one of them was their father Luke. The twins hardly recognized him. He didn't have a beard and he wasn't wearing his thick jam jar glasses. He looked strong and confident. He looked like a leader, someone who makes decisions and not at all like the father at home who can't even remember the twins' birthday.

"She's given her order," their father said. "You know what has to be done."

The two men from the truck were now running towards the prisoner.

"Noooooooooo," they both shouted, trying to stand between the prisoner and Luke.

"He would never betray us."

"He's not a traitor," they yelled.

"He's been set up."

There were people everywhere all yelling and there was a lot of pushing. Tensions seemed to be reaching boiling point. The twins could tell that it was all about to kick off. Tempers started getting heated and voices were getting louder and louder.

"Look at the facts," one man said. "Only he knew the coordinates, no one else. How did the Germans find out? Who led them there? He did it because he's a traitor."

"No, he's not," another person screamed.

The twins feared for their and their father's life.

"We've gotta get out of here, now!" Aramis yelled to Kat over all of the screaming, but Kat was too scared to move.

"Noooooooooo," screamed the lady from the village. "He didn't do anything. He's been set up."

As the men dragged the prisoner past the twins still standing in the tunnel, the prisoner turned back as if to get another look at them. He seemed to smile. The woman was screaming hysterically and then the twins heard gunshots. People were running everywhere. They couldn't see their father.

"Dad!" Kat screamed but her voice was drowned by others screaming above her.

The twins turned to run, and although still feeling groggy from being drugged, there was no way they were staying there. They managed to move back toward the entrance of the cave. They could see that it was getting lighter and then they heard voices behind them and running. They were being chased. *Not again*, Aramis thought.

However, in all of the commotion, the prisoner had somehow escaped and was sprinting towards them. He pushed Kat up against the wall and said, "Don't trust anyone other than him," pointing at Aramis. Kat felt something being pushed into her hand, something small and rough. *Paper*, she thought.

"And don't show anyone your crystals. Especially your parents." The prisoner then did something that startled them even more. If that was at all possible.

They thought they saw him throw something into the air. It looked like a scrunched up piece of paper, and then he ran into it and disappeared. He literally just ran into the paper and disappeared. The twins looked at each other in disbelief.

"Did you see that?" Aramis said out of the corner of his mouth Kat nodded. "I think so."

"Okay, I've been drugged," Aramis said.

With their backs still up against the cave, a crowd started to gather around the entrance of the cave looking for signs of the prisoner. Not believing what they had both seen and putting it down to being drugged, they were feeling exhausted and overwhelmed. A whirlwind of emotions flooded over them.

Kat vaguely heard someone ask what happened and then everyone turned and looked at the twins.

"What are you two doing here?" a lady's voice yelled.

"It's okay, they're with me." a second voice called out.

Scared and tired, they daren't look to see whom the second voice belonged to. A person from the crowd moved forward.

"Mum? Is that you?" Kat said, hardly believing her eyes.

In front of them was their mother. Although scarcely recognizable, she was there. Her hair brushed and pinned back into victory rolls. She looked like one of those ladies that Kat had seen pictures of that were painted on the sides of airplanes.

There were no glasses in sight and she was wearing tan-coloured overalls with a tan-coloured jacket with a fur trim collar, dark brown boots, and dark brown leather gloves. A pair of goggles hung around her neck.

"Mum, are you a pilot?" Kat asked.

"She's gone," a voice in the crowd said. "She must've slipped out in all of the chaos."

"What's happening?" Luke pushed through the crowd towards Ashleigh, "Holy cow, what are you guys doing here? How on earth..."

"They're both okay," Ashleigh said to Luke.

"They both got away," he said to Ashleigh.

"So this is what you guys do every second weekend?" Aramis said. "Couldn't you just do cosplay?" He laughed. "Can we go home?"

"I think that's a great idea," Ashleigh said, hugging the kids. "You two have really had an adventure, haven't you?"

"I'd just like to forget all about it to be honest," Aramis said, walking beside his dad.

"So let's talk about you guys and your double life," Aramis said, looking at his parents in complete and utter awe.

"What? No more being called vegan bike-riding hippies?" Luke said, jokingly to Aramis

Aramis for once looked embarrassed.

"Come on, mate, we've got a lot to talk about," Luke said, putting his arm around his son. "Starting with, how on earth you two got here."

Kat kept the paper tightly balled up in her hand, wondering what could be written on it.

PART THREE

NEW ZEALAND
1863

CHAPTER TEN

"Well, at least it's getting easier, mate." Aramis turned to Kat who was still doubled over ready to vomit. "You just need to remember to breathe. Where's the map?" he asked.

Kat pulled the map from her bag. The crumpled up map was what the prisoner had pushed into her hand back in 1944 in the cave. She remembered it so vividly. His dark brown eyes looked intensely at her. She was terrified but she felt safe at the same time. She trusted him. She trusted him so much that she didn't even tell her parents about the map or what he had said to her. She knew those eyes from somewhere. She just couldn't put her finger on it, but she knew him, and worse, she trusted him as much as she trusted her twin Aramis.

After they'd gotten home that night from being in France 1944, after they had talked with their parents about how the twins had got there, after their parents who led this secret double life had tucked them up into bed - the twins made their own plan. A plan that involved the crystals and the map that the prisoner had given them. And finding pieces of the star. And putting them back together.

"Okay, so what do we know? When are we?" Aramis said, looking around at the huge canopy of trees above him. The morning dew was still settling on the leaves and glistened in the early morning sun as it stretched into the sky. The leaves under his feet crunched softly with every move. A Tui sang a familiar song above them.

"Well, we're still in NZ, which rocks," he said, looking up at the Tui. "Why didn't we just ask Lu to drive us to the Waikato? We live maybe an hour an hour and half away sooooo ..."

Kat stood up now fully recovered. No matter how much she did it, traveling through the tunnel always made her feel sick. But Aramis was right, it was getting slightly easier.

"We know the location, but we don't know the time and actually the Waikato is vast."

The twins looked around. They seemed to be in the middle of a forest. They were surrounded by thick bushes. The twins looked like ants besides the majestic Kauri, Rimu and Totara trees towering above them. The ground was moist and covered in deep vegetation. And the ground climbed high behind them and sloped below them. They were in the middle of the ancient forest.

"I just hope it isn't that forest that is said to be haunted. Spirits run through singing a high-pitch screeching wail, like a banshee. One of them wearing an orange red cloak and the other is carrying a carved wooden box."

"Oooo," Aramis joked, shaking his hands and wriggling his fingers at Kat pretending to be a ghost "Spooookyy."

"Hey, everything has a basis in something! Let's just hope it's not that forest."

"Seriously?" Aramis rolled his eyes.

"Oh, be quiet," Kat said.

Suddenly there were loud bangs. Gunshots.

"What the hell is that?" Aramis said. "Was that a gunshot?"

As they looked to see where the gunshots were coming from, they saw a flash of reddish orange between the green vegetation below them farther down the hill. Then behind them, they heard the sound of some sort of horn farther up the hill.

"This can't be good," Aramis said, quickly surveying the area around them.

As the twins looked around, they just knew that something or someone would be heading right up that hill toward them. They could faintly hear something moving fast toward them. They could hear shouting and then more gunshots also heading up the hill. They were chasing something and they didn't seem at all happy about it.

The twins could feel something getting closer. Still looking down the hill Kat started stepping backward.

"Urrrgghhh!" she screamed.

She had tripped and fell back into a hole in the ground. It wasn't an exceptionally large hole. In fact, if she hadn't have fallen into it, the twins wouldn't have even noticed it. It was a shallow hole, similar to an old food pit, that was completely covered by an old Totara tree that must've fallen over it years before. It was just deep enough for the twins to stand up in it and the Totara provided a type of natural roofing above. Overtime ferns and other plants had grown on top of the old tree providing the perfect camouflage.

"Kat," Aramis said above the hole. "Are you okay?"

"I am," she said, brushing herself off.

Aramis, knowing something was heading up the hill, climbed down into the hole. It was perfectly hidden. Inside the hole, the twins could hear something running.

Their hearts pounding louder and louder, they both turned towards a small opening of light at the top of the hole. Kat grabbed hold of Aramis's arm. They could hear the running slowing and a lot of people shouting as they pursued whatever was near them.

In the distance above them, they heard a horn sound two times then panting. They could hear panting and it was close, too close. Kat and Aramis backed right up against the back of the hole.

Their backs up against the moist earth, Kat wished that she and Aramis could dissolve right into it. She held on even tighter to Aramis's arm.

Scarcely breathing, the twins knew that someone or something was just outside the hole. Then they saw feet. Human feet and legs. The person then reached into the hole, searching for something. The person's hand ran along a tree root searching out exactly what they needed. They were so close that the twins could feel their heavy breath on their faces.

"Where is it?" a male voice said. A deep rough voice, he had clearly left something there. Then his hand grasped something. As he pulled it out into the sunlight, it glistened as only Pounamu could. It was a Pounamu Patu and then he reached back in for something else. Kat could see what he was searching for. She could see a long stick-like shape in the darkness of the hole. It must've fallen from where he had left it in the tree root and was inches in front of her feet. Although she was scared, she knew that if she didn't move it closer to the man, he would come into the hole. That stick was obviously important. He couldn't linger for much longer and obviously needed it.

Kat slowly pushed the stick closer to the opening with her foot. The top of the stick was sticking up through the root and just needed the bottom of the stick to somehow be lifted up. She moved slowly and with her foot quietly nudged the stick up.

"Argh, there you are." As the man grabbed hold of it, he pulled it out. Kat got a closer look at it. It wasn't a stick made of wood. It was a Taiaha. It was intricately carved. Kat could see that this Taiaha wasn't made of wood. It was a light colour, and she remembered seeing one just like that on a school trip to the museum. It was made of bone. Whalebone. The Taiaha that she had seen at the museum was hundreds of years old. This one was new.

Having retrieved the Patu and Taiaha, the man ran off, making his way up the hill behind them. They could hear a group chasing him and more gunshots being fired. Adrenaline raced through them but the twins stayed frozen in the hole until they were sure that the danger had passed.

"Get the map out and let's see where the crystal is. The sooner we get outta here the better," Aramis said.

Kat pulled the map from her bag and hung her crystal over it. The map sprung into life, showing a path to a marae straight up the hill behind them.

"Are you mad? There's no way I'm going up there with whoever has those guns."

"The map shows another way. We have to follow a stream or river and then hike back up the mountain through the bush on the other side," Kat said, looking down the hill and then looking back up. They could still hear shouting and gunfire farther up above them.

"Okey-dokey, downhill it is," Kat said, packing the map into her satchel.

They made their way steadily down through the thick forest. "I can see how someone could really get lost and die here, no one would ever find you. We're like right out in the wops. When do you think we are, y'know, like what year?"

"Yes, I know, the forest is so thick and it's really disorientating. The daylight is hardly coming through the canopy, at a guess, I'd say 1900's? Maybe."

The river came into view twisted through the dense bush. Following the river and still trying to figure out "when they were," Aramis's mind flicked to their parents.

"Can you believe that Mum and Dad have been travelling back and forth through time to WW2 and Mum was actually a fighter pilot? Our Mum! I mean she's so cool and they fought with the white mouse. They joined the resistance. They are pretty darn cool," Aramis said proudly.

"Okay, did you just say Mum and Dad and cool in the same sentence?" Kat teased. "So they're no longer the bike-riding vegan wannabe hippies?" she said, laughing.

"All of that was a disguise. I can't believe it. But who was that man and woman who seemed to know us? All Mum and Dad said was that they were very bad people, time walkers. They belong to the order of Isaiah and are trying to undo time and erase history and need the Star of Peace."

"They betrayed the resistance. The white mouse needed to find out who the traitor was. I thought that was pretty clever of her to give each of her team fake coordinates, aye. At least that way only she would know who the traitor was once the Germans arrived at the wrong rendezvous. They used up a lot of resources but it had to be done, hundreds had died because of the traitor and the white mouse had almost been caught."

"Yes, I know, but if the prisoner and the lady from the village were so bad, why didn't they kill us? And how did they know us? I mean she kissed my head and he shoved that map into my hand, my hand, not Mum's or Dad's and he said to only trust you, but I don't know. What if he was set up and someone else other than he gave the coordinates. It doesn't make sense."

The twins followed the river for close to an hour and decided to stop to check their map and the location of the next piece of the star. The crystal glowed as Kat held hers above the map. An image started to appear, like before it showed a Pā high on a hill with a long river below winding around to the left of the hill. The map showed the general location of where they were and then how far away the new crystal was. It showed it as a pulsating beep that looked like a heartbeat.

"Okay, so it's back up there but the other path is over that way," Kat said, folding the map back up and putting it back in her bag.

"Well, we better get a move on, I don't want to be around when whoever has those guns come back," said Aramis.

There was a snap of a twig. The twins whirled around looking for the cause of it.

"When who comes back?" a voice behind them said.

CHAPTER ELEVEN

The twins turned and were face to face with men dressed in blue uniforms. They could hear a clunking noise and muffled voices in the distance. And before they knew it, they were surrounded by more soldiers in blue uniforms.

"I thought they wore red uniforms. They always have red uniforms on TV," Aramis said to Kat as the soldiers surrounded them.

One of the soldiers looked at the twins in disgust like they were something that had been vomited up. They were told to walk and the twins were not about to argue with hostile armed soldiers. The soldiers in their blue uniforms were not at all what Aramis and Kat had expected. They had thought from TV and movies that the soldiers were well-mannered, kind-hearted humanitarians. The opposite was more true.

"We must be in the 1800's probably mid to late," Kat said as they walked.

"Shut it!" a soldier said in a thick cockney accent, pushing their backs with the butt of his rifle.

"Bloody savages," another said under his breath. *Savages?* Aramis mouthed to Kat. The twins walked along the stream surrounded by the soldiers until a clearing came into sight. There, they came across a sea of white canvas tents. All in uniform rows averaging twenty-five to thirty-five tents per row, and the twins could see at least fifteen rows.

The mud-trodden ground lined a well-worn path of wagon wheels to a larger tent towards the middle of the rows. The ground, still damp from the morning dew, looked as if it had received heavy rain recently.

The soldiers were shocked that the twins spoke English given their "colouring". A soldier referred to them as being bronze savages and another called them a pair of dirty heathens and that the twins were obviously educated by missionaries. Aramis frowned but Kat reminded him to stay on track and that the soldiers only knew what they knew. It's not their fault, and given the time they were in, racism was considered normal.

Squishing through the mud they were led to the larger tent, thrown in and advised to stay and not to touch anything. As they stood there they could hear soldiers talking about a captain who had apparently been questioned over his relationship with a Māori female. He would probably be court-marshalled and sent back to Britain to stand trial for his disgusting behavior. She was also being held and it was her brother who was being chased up the hill when the twins arrived. Her brother was trying to break her out but was unsuccessful and more guards had been put on the tent of where she was.

"Who are you and what are you doing in my camp?" a stern voice behind them commanded. The twins turned around to find a man with dark hair with gray flecks, with piercing green eyes staring straight at them.

"Well, speak now!" he abruptly commanded again. "Who are you?"

Kat could sense Aramis starting to tense up as following directions or orders was not something that he ever did, and this man seemed like a grouchy impatient principal.

"Hello, my name is Kat and this is my brother, Aramis. We were just passing by and stumbled upon your soldiers."

"Why!" He demanded.

The twins looked puzzled - "Why?"

"Why are you here?"

"Ummmm, because we were walking and came across your soldiers and they made us come here."

"And you just happened to come to my camp? Again I ask, why? Why are you here? To break that savage out like that so-called warrior?" he said in a patronizing voice.

Kat and Aramis looked at each other. Aramis was about to blurt into one of his rants when there was more shouting outside.

"Stay there," the man ordered, pointing his finger at the twins, "and don't touch anything." He stormed out of the tent.

"What the hell is going on now?" they heard him yell.

"Well," Aramis said, looking at Kat, "as I'm not one to listen, there is no way I'm waiting for him to get back."

Kat agreed and they decided to climb under the edge of the tent at the back. Before leaving, Aramis noticed the perfectly ordered desk with everything in its place. With the voice of the grouchy General Jack Browne still ringing in his mind, "Don't touch anything," Aramis couldn't stop himself from moving everything on the desk, from ordered to complete chaos. With a satisfied smirk on his face they scrambled out the back of the tent.

As they came out from under the tent, they came face to face with a pair of boots that were attached to a soldier looking down at them. "God, it just gets better," Aramis said sarcastically, standing upright looking defiantly at the soldier.

CHAPTER TWELVE

"I'm guessing you're trying to escape from General Jack Browne?" the soldier asked. "You better come this way then. And keep your head down so no one sees you."

"Huh?" Aramis looked at Kat. "You're gonna help us?"

"Just keep your head down," the soldier ordered.

As they navigated their way around the back of the camp, the twins were thankful that most of the soldiers were gathered around closer to the General's tent. The area backed onto forest and the twins were not thrilled to stay any longer in the camp than necessary.

"It looks like the troops have returned unsuccessful from chasing Wairakas brother, Kaiahi."

"Wairaka? Is she the lady that is being held in the tent next to the General's?" Kat asked.

"Yes, she is. Her brother Kaiahi is determined to break her free. I don't know how that will be possible. The general has moved her right beside his tent and has doubled the guards," he said.

"Why are they holding her?" Kat inquired.

"Well, first of all, she is the daughter of a chief. A chief who will not work or even compromise with the general. Secondly, she is in love with someone that, according to the general and British military law, she shouldn't be in love with as she is apparently beneath him."

"Beneath him?"

"Yes, he's an English officer and she's..."

"She's Māori?"

"Yes...she's Māori."

"And that's a crime?" Aramis chimed in. "You do know you're in New Zealand? Māori are Tangata whenua," he said.

"Hmmm, I may have heard something like that," the soldier said, smiling at them. "By the way, my name is Darcy Drummond. Very pleased to make your acquaintance," he said, shaking their hands. "And you are?"

"I'm Aramis and this is my sister, Kat."

"And why are you here, of all places? What made you come here?"

"It's a long story and I don't think that you have enough time to hear it all," Kat said.

"Why are you helping us?" Aramis asked as they were running towards the forest.

"Haven't you guessed? I'm not exactly the best captain in this camp."

Suddenly it all made sense to Kat. This soldier wasn't any soldier. This was the English officer - Wairaka's officer.

Looking at the ground, he looked heartbroken. "You see, I love her. I truly love her. If you met her, you would love her too. She's so strong and determined. And she's fiery as well. She just has such a strong presence that when I met her, my heart was committed to her from that moment on. I was told that if I don't end it, that I will be decommissioned and sent home in shame. Well, I'm not bloody ending it! How can you end something that is part of you? She's part of me, part of my total being, my soul. She's my everything you know. Just my everything," he gushed.

"Can I ask a favor of you?" he begged. "I understand if you can't do it but if you could...I wonder...could you possibly, could you go to Wairakas' brother, Kaiahi? Could you tell him where Wairaka is? Tell him that Darcy sent you. I will try to get her free but you need to get a message to him. I will make sure that we will get back to the

Pā. Kaiahi just has to create another distraction and I'll get her out then," he said. "Now go. Please find them. Just follow the ridgeline. I have to get back before I'm missed," he said as he ran back towards the other soldiers.

The twins ran as fast as they could, desperate to get away from the camp. They found the stream that they had originally followed and ran along it - back towards where they had originally come from. As they neared the fallen totara tree and hole that they hid in, they heard the horn again.

They looked at each other with complete dread. But Aramis could see the spark of an idea forming in Kat's head.

"No no no no no!" Aramis said, looking at Kat. "We are here to find the crystal and not be someone's messenger. Secondly, we have no idea where the Pā is and then ... Well, look at us. Look at how we're dressed. We can't just rock on up to the Pā and say, 'Heyyyyyyyy s'up, bro, so no!"

"I know, but Darcy looked sad, heartbrokenly sad, and he helped us escape. We owe him. We really do."

"I don't care" Aramis muttered "I really don't and I'm pretty sure we can't just go around changing people's destinies, can we?"

"Oh, stop it. We're here so we may as well try. I'll make you a deal...If we walk up to the top along the ridge and we don't find Kaiahi..."

"Or he doesn't find us." Aramis interrupted

"Okay, or he doesn't find us then we will follow the map and retrieve the crystal and leave, deal?"

"Deal!"

With that the twins walked towards the top of the ridgeline towards where they thought that they had heard the horn sounding.

"Okay, so we're here, and yep, there's no one here so let's get back to the map," Aramis said, puffing. "Man, I am so unfit - that Kaiahi dude must be fit as, because he sprinted up this hill."

"Probably all of those pies you keep shoving in your gob," Kat said smiling, reaching in her bag for the map.

"Right so the map is taking us to the left, which is along this ridgeline" Aramis said. "What's the plan?"

"Well," Kat said, looking around. She inched closer to Aramis and whispered "You know that feeling you have when you are being watched?"

They both looked at each other and then looked up. Looking down on them was a pair of deep dark brown eyes. A man jumped down from the tree above and landed in front of them. He wasn't the man with the Taiaha. That man had tattoos all the way down his legs to his feet. This man didn't.

He had a shell in his hand that had a carved wooden mouthpiece at the end.

He peered at the twins with an untrusting stare then put the horn to his lips. He blew that horn with two short bursts. Shortly after, they heard rustling all around them. They looked at each other.

Again the twins were surrounded by men that they didn't know. Men who did not know them and men who didn't trust them. Aramis slumped on the ground - "Man, we never get a break do we?" he muttered under his breath.

"Kaiahi?" Kat asked. "Do you know Kaiahi," she said optimistically. "Kaiahi," she said, turning in almost a full circle facing Taiahas pointing directly at her and Aramis.

"Kaiahi, what do you want with Kaiahi. Did the Pākeha send you?" a man demanded. He had a tattoo across the lower part of his face that finished just below his eyes. He was fierce-looking, tall, and strong. A true warrior.

Kat was a petite little thing, but she always held her own. She was like one of those pictures that showed a cat looking in the mirror and only saw a lion. That was her, a lion. Shoulders back, she stepped forward and said strongly, "Darcy Drummond sent us and said that Wai will be safe and he will get her out."

With that, the warrior grabbed Kats' arm. Aramis protectively lunged forward only to be forced back by another warrior.

"You better get your hands off my sister, mate," he said.

"Or what? What will you do, boy?" the warrior mocked.

"Ohhhhh no," Kat said, shaking her head. She knew without a doubt that if there was one thing Aramis hated being called was 'boy'.

"So what, boy, what are you going to do?" he said, shoving Aramis backwards with his face so close to Aramis that Aramis could see the blood vessels in his eyes.

Kat could feel tension rise between Aramis and the warriors. *Great,* she thought, *it's all about to kick-off!*

Just then another warrior appeared. This warrior, again tall and athletic looking, had a full Ta Moko on his face and tattoos on his arms and legs that went all the way down to his feet. He walked towards the twins.

"Who are you?" he said, holding his Taiaha to Aramis.

"They said that Darcy sent them."

"You have spoken with Darcy. Did he tell you of my sister?"

"Are you the people of the clouds from the heavens?" another warrior asked.

"Yes, he said to let you know that she has been moved closer to the general's tent and there are more soldiers guarding her," Kat said. "And no, sorry we are not the people from the heavens. I don't know who they are sorry."

Kaiahi sighed, kicking the ground with his bare feet. "Matenga," he said. "You, Parahi, and Te Whao will go to Tamainupō and figure out our next move to get her back. I will go to Whaea Pania and let her know what's going on."

"And those two? Matenga said.

"I'll take these two with me. See what Whaea makes of them," he said, turning his back.

Matenga was the warrior that had mocked Aramis and called him boy. He turned and purposely pushed his shoulder into Aramis, saying, "I'll see you later, *boy*," before strutting away.

The tension between the warriors and the twins seemed to follow them as they were forced to sprint up, over and along the ridgeline through the dense forest.

When Kat thought that she could no longer run any farther, Kaiahi slowed down to a jogging pace and then finally slowed to a walking pace.

The twins were sweating and thought that their lungs were ready to burst. Kaiahi was completely unaware of the fact that fitness was not their usual regime and looked at them as if they were the most useless excuse for human beings he had ever had to lay his eyes on.

The thick dense forest started thinning out, and a small wooden a-frame building came into sight. It looked as if it was half buried into the earth as there were mounds of earth up against the sides of the building.

The twins had seen whares before. Maraes and Pās are commonplace in New Zealand but this one was different. It wasn't inside a Pā. It was on its own. It looked enchantingly beautiful. The wood looked like it was Kauri and was a warm mellow yellowish colour.

The whare had a low door in the front and a smallish single window to the side of the door. The barge boards were heavily carved, but not how the twins had ever seen carved before. Usually, where the barge boards meet would normally be a Taniwha type figure, but on this whare, was a Merkaba. The twins knew this Merkaba well. It was the same one that was on the Book of Peace. Surrounding the Merkaba were swirls twisting and turning and below that were the eight phases of the moon ending with a large sunburst. The barge boards themselves had constellations carved down both sides, surrounded in more swirls that seemed to represent celestial bodies. It seemed so modern. Something you would expect in the 2020's at a modern expo.

The roof was covered in vegetation. Dirt must have been put on top at some stage and now ferns grew. It was very natural and extremely beautiful. There was mist around the whare, which made it look even more magical. Encircling the whare was a fence made of twisted and thwarted branches, interspersed with carvings of female warriors, which were not different in themselves; however, they were not facing outward. Instead they faced inward as if watching over the whare.

A lady came out of the whare and motioned them towards her. She was tall and wore a cloak around her shoulders, not a feathered cloak, but one that was finely woven of fiber with fiber tassels covering it. The cloak covered her body, and as she moved, her piupiu showed.

Her chin and lips were tattooed with a moko, and her long dark wavy hair hung down past her shoulders and had three feathers on top of her head.

"This is Whaea Pania," Kaiahi said, looking at the twins. "My father's sister. She's a healer and a seer. She is revered in our family. Don't say anything," he hissed towards the twins and walked in front of them.

CHAPTER THIRTEEN

Surprisingly, Aramis didn't react. He didn't say anything back. He just walked quietly towards the whare, dissecting every part of the architecture, as if he were devouring a delicious 5-star dinner. It was certainly a feast for the eyes.

The twins followed behind Kaiahi and stopped to remove their shoes before entering. They felt safe for the first time since they had arrived. Maybe seeing the Merkaba somehow made them feel safe.

Inside was dark as there was only one window and one door but it was still light enough to see. There was a fire in the middle and a small hole in the roof to let the smoke out. Inside there were baskets of plants and leaves. The two central posts of the whare were again carved with stars, planets, and moons in different phases and the sun. The twins knew she must be the holder of the crystal.

It was so out of the ordinary that the twins didn't know what to expect. The twins had grown up in New Zealand. Māori heritage is an integral part of living in NZ. It's something that is in your everyday life but this whare was something different. It was magical, but not scary religious fear-based magical. It was a loving magical, and the twins reveled in it.

They respectfully stood well back from Kaiahi as he spoke with Whaea Pania. Behind them a younger lady pushed past carrying a kete filled with berries and food.

"Hello," she said. She was also tall and athletic and very beautiful. She pressed her forehead and nose to Kat first and then to Aramis. She had a light sprinkling of freckles just across the bridge of her nose. You could see the family resemblance between her, Kaiahi, Whaea Pania, and the warriors. She looked at least nineteen or twenty years old.

"I am Te Miringa. Are you the children of the heavens?" she asked, looking at both of them smilingly handing them both berries from her kete. "Are you hungry?" she asked.

"Children of the heavens?"

"Yes, Whaea Pania has spoken about two visitors that would one day come for the blue stone. Is that you? Our family have been guardians of the stone for a very long time. Your story has been one that has been told to generation after generation by our ancestors."

"Our story? We have a story?" Kat whispered

"You were expecting us?"

"Yes, we've been expecting you for generations. You are from the heavens, from another place. We've been told how you will walk through from the stars and save what is close to our hearts. I can't believe that you are finally here standing with me," she said excitingly. "I am being trained by Whaea to learn about you, so now I suppose I won't be learning anymore." She laughed.

"Miri," Whaea Pania said, "leave our guests. Please come," she said, motioning for the twins to move closer to her and Kaiahi.

Kaiahi looked worried. He turned to leave. "I'll bring the others back soon," he said.

Whaea Pania nodded and turned her attention to the twins. After welcoming the twins into her whare, Whaea Pania said, "You are the children of the heavens, aren't you? Of the stars? We have waited for you for a long time. This is my nephew, Ruapane."

A gorgeous little boy ran in and out of the whare, playing. Kat and Aramis watched as he seemed to be talking to someone that they couldn't see.

Seeing Kat's curiosity Whaea Pania explained, "He plays and speaks with the children of our ancestors, of those who have gone before us."

Kat smiled and said, "Yes, we are. Yes, we are the children of the stars."

Aramis watched Kaiahi walk out of the whare. "He's worried about his sister, Wairaka. He's trying to work out a way to rescue her. He's a very fierce warrior, very quick and loves his sister. She is also a warrior. She is very talented but the Pākeha have weapons that are not like ours. They have different ways of thinking and acting. Kaiahi fights with honor. They do not have honor. I worry that he will attack again and will fight with his heart for his sister and not his head," she said, sighing.

"But this is not your problem. We have kept the stone safe for you," she said, bringing out a beautifully carved box.

Kat gasped. It was the box from Lu's house.

"But how?" she asked. "How is this possible?"

"This was carved by my great-grandfather, Te Houpapa. Have you seen it before?"

"Yes, yes, I have. Look, Aramis," Kat said, turning to Aramis. But Aramis was still looking out the whare door.

As Kat opened the box, she found another blue crystal, and under it was another piece of the map. She pulled out hers from her bag and the tear marks matched perfectly. Kat whispered to herself, *I don't understand. This must've been the map that the prisoner had, so how did it get here?*

Aramis had finally looked away from the whare door.

"Are you okay?" Kat asked Aramis.

"Yeah, yeah, I am. Just ... I know how Kaiahi feels. When we were in France, I was so worried about you. I will do anything to keep you safe." he shrugged and looked at the box Kat had been given.

Whaea Pania continued her story "Generations ago, a warrior from the stars came. He told us of you two one day coming to us. He gave my ancestor Huingariri the stone and that," Whaea Pania said, pointing at the map, "but as a thank-you for guarding the stone, he also gave us the gift of the red cloak and the white taiaha. We have treasured these for centuries."

"Really, did he say who he was? His name?"

"We know him as Addie, the warrior of the star."

"Addie, oh okay, thank you."

Kaiahi, Matenga, Parahi and Te Whao returned.

"We have decided to strike tonight," Kaiahi said. "They won't be expecting a hit again so soon."

"Tonight?" Whaea Pania asked. "Is that wise? Wait for the others to arrive. We have sent word to other tribes to help. They should be here soon. Tautari, Kore, and Merepatene are also coming. We will be better equipped."

"Yes, but every day we waste is a day longer that she has to suffer. She is strong but I don't know if she is strong enough to handle the torture. You didn't see her. She was beaten and tied up. Her eyes were swollen. She couldn't see me. I was so close to her, then those soldiers arrived. I can't just leave her there. I can't. I have to do something."

Aramis was standing, staring at Kat. Kat looked at him and shook her head. She knew what he was thinking.

"No," she whispered.

"I have to," he said, holding out his arms to her.

Panic once again creeped along Kat's veins. "No! What happened to messing with other's destinies, and you are the one that said we are just here for the crystal. Well, here's the crystal. We've got it. We can go," she pleaded.

"No, we can't go," he said softly. "They need more people and I know the layout of the camp and exactly where she is. I'll have my crystal so we will be safe, okay? We will be safe," he said, hugging Kat. "But I have to help. It's his sister."

Realising she would never win this argument Kat said "Please be safe, please. I couldn't handle anything happening to you. Don't go doing any kung fu karate rubbish and being the hero. It's not TV. Please, Aramis, please be safe."

"Will you help us?" Kaiahi said.

Aramis nodded his head.

Matenga stood behind him and said, "I'll be watching you, boy."

"Glad to hear it," said Aramis, still hugging Kat.

"Leave him alone," Te Whao said. "We need all the help we can get to get Wai out tonight."

"It's not just Wai, it's Darcy as well. They are going to make him lead them to us, and if he doesn't, well ... we have to get him as well. Plus I wouldn't want to be the one to tell Wai that we forgot him, would you?" Kaiahi laughed. "Let's just say she wouldn't be at all happy."

"I don't know where his tent is," Aramis said in a panic.

"I do," Parahi said

"Good, then Parahi, you, and Te Whao go for Darcy and us three will go for Wai. As soon as you get him, come straight back here."

"You'll need this," Kat said to Aramis, reaching into her bag. She pulled out a torch.

"Really, why?"

"Yes really, what did you think I was going to do? Pull out a magic wand or something?" She laughed. "They don't have torches; they only have fire, candles, and oil lamps. That'll freak them out. It's got multi-colour strobe lights on it as well. It may give you guys more time, and take a cellphone."

"Whhhhaaaattt? What for? To call for backup? Ummm, yeah, can you come to 1860 something just past the punga stump near the stream and help a brother out?" he joked back.

"No, you clown to play some music and turn the light on the phone on as well. It's dark and they are pretty superstitious, so it may help, and take these Bluetooth speakers. They may be small but they pack a punch," she said. "Do you have your pocket knife?"

"Yep, got it."

"Alrighty then, good to go," she said, hugging Aramis and checking that he had his crystal with him. "Sync all of the speakers to the cellphone and blast some music. Seriously, it will freak them completely out."

"You're pretty clever, sis."

The warriors all looked at each other completely puzzled, having no idea what Kat had just given Aramis.

The five waited until it was dark and left Whaea Panias whare, racing down the ridge back toward the camp. They were swift and even Aramis could keep up, although he briefly wondered how he was going to go running at the same speed going back up the hill.

CHAPTER FOURTEEN

It was now dark with the moon rising higher into the night sky, Aramis watched as the moon illuminated all that it touched. He was surprised by the amount that he could actually see by moonlight. They made it down to the edge of the forest. Parahi and Te Whao split off and headed to Darcy.

"Her tent is over there right next to the big tent," Aramis whispered to Kaiahi.

There were soldiers out the front of the tent and Kaiahi, Aramis, and Matenga could see around the back. No one was at the back. They were guarding the front.

"It's too easy. There should be guards at the back. It's a trap!" Aramis said.

"What? What do you mean? We can go through the back to get her."

"No. I think they've either moved her or someone is inside with her."

They scanned the rest of the camp, looking for tents with more than one guard on it. But there weren't any other tents with guards except for the one that Wairaka was in during the day.

"Let me crawl over there and listen to see if there's anyone inside," Matenga said.

"Okay, but the first sign of any soldiers, you get out of there straight away." Matenga nodded.

"Can you take one of these with you?" Aramis asked, handing a Bluetooth speaker to him. "Just put it on the ground near the tent," he said. Matenga shrugged, he had no idea what this weird thing was. "Trust me" Aramis whispered. With that Matenga moved off.

Aramis and Kaiahi waited at the edge of the forest crouched down low. Adrenaline pumped through his veins but Aramis did not have a good feeling. The camp was too quiet. There were a few fires and they could see a couple of guards, but there were at least two hundred soldiers in that camp, so where were they all?

"I say we go as soon as Matenga comes back."

"No," Aramis said. "The camp is too quiet. There are close to two hundred soldiers, and camps are never this quiet. Something is going on. They're waiting for us."

The camp was to the front of them, and Aramis and Kaiahi heard noises to the side of where they were. Their adrenaline was really running now. "Shhhhhh," Kaiahi said, pointing to the left of them. They briefly saw a flash of silver in the moonlight.

Aramis turned to look for Matenga. He couldn't see him but they could see soldiers positioning themselves between where they were and the camp, and they knew that Matenga would be heading back this way. It was an ambush. And Matenga was going to walk right into the trap.

We've got to do something, Aramis thought. *Matenga is going to come straight back into the soldiers.* Aramis's mind was racing. He felt sick. *How can I distract them and lead them away?* he thought. *What if I go back slightly up the hill to the left and play some music and shine the torch? It's so quiet and hearing heavy metal will alert Matenga to stay where he is and give the soldiers' positions away or maybe scare them.* That was the only thing he could think of. Normally Kat was the one with the plans.

Aramis whispered his plan to Kaiahi. Kaiahi didn't like it, but they had to do something to save Matenga.

Aramis quietly moved away heading farther up the hill. He knew that sound would travel. He positioned one Bluetooth speaker at the base of a tree and turned it on, then ran about a hundred meters higher and placed the other speaker down. He had left one with Kaiahi and Matenga had one. *That should just about do it*, he thought. If he could play some heavy metal, it should distract the soldiers long enough for Matenga to get back safely. He reached into his pocket and realized that he had Kat's phone.

Oh my god, he thought. "Her music is rubbish," he mumbled to himself. Then he saw the only download she had other than meditations. It was a download of relaxing whale sounds. *Oh great*, he thought to himself. *Great, we'll bore them to death.*

He climbed the tree to get a better look at the soldier's locations. He linked the phone to the speakers. And with nothing else to lose and no better music options he pressed play. The sound of whales roared so loud through the quiet forest he could have sworn that they were right there beside him. He could see the soldiers starting to move, looking around. He turned the volume up slightly on the phone and whale sounds boomed throughout the forest. It sounded eerie as it echoed down through the forest into the camp as if hundreds of spirits were coming straight for the camp. He set his torch to strobe and different colours flicked on and off. He waved the torch around in the hopes that it would scare the soldiers. He turned the volume up as loud as it could go and saw the soldiers running terrified back to the camp. It worked.

"Well, what do you know? Kat was right," he said quite chuffed.

The soldiers had moved and Matenga could come back safe. Aramis sat up in the tree looking for any stragglers still making their way back to camp, and by the time he got back to Kaiahi, Matenga was back. Matenga said that when he got to the tent, he realized that it was a trap. There were soldiers inside with Wairaka. Then all those spirit sounds started and spooked the soldiers inside the tent. They ran out and Matenga managed to get inside.

"I saw her. She's pretty bad, Kaiahi. She's tied up with her arms above her head and she's been beaten badly. Her head was hanging down. She was covered in blood."

In the night light, Aramis could see the desperation on Kaiahi's face. "I'm going to get her. I have to," he said. "You two stay here."

"No, no," Matenga said, putting his hand up to stop Kaiahi.

Just then, they heard, "NOOOOOOOOOOOOOOOOOOOOOO, you bloody imbeciles!" coming from the camp. Aramis, Kaiahi, and Matenga looked back toward the camp. "Time to go," Matenga growled, pulling Kaiahi away. The three ran back up along the ridgeline. It was surprising just how fast Aramis could run when he thought that he was being chased.

CHAPTER FIFTEEN

They made it back to Whaea Panias whare just as it was starting to get light and walked in. Kaiahi lingered outside, disappointed that he hadn't returned with his little sister. His heart was breaking, knowing that she had been tortured. He felt completely and utterly powerless and overwhelmed with guilt. He stood outside looking back in the direction of the camp. He felt his aunty touch his arm.

"I'm sorry, Whaea. I didn't bring her back. I couldn't get to her. I don't know how to save her," he said with a lump in his throat. The last time he had felt like this was when his mother Tukotuku had passed away. He was overcome with grief then, and now grief had crept back into his life.

Kaiahi and Wairaka had fought over her choice to love Darcy. Kaiahi had disagreed and forbade Wairaka to ever see him again. Wairaka, being Wairaka, completely ignored Kaiahi and told him that she would see whomever she liked whenever she liked. She defiantly told Kaiahi that she loved Darcy and that if he couldn't accept him then she would go and live with him and the Pākeha.

That was the last time Kaiahi saw her. She left to be with Darcy, but what Wairaka didn't know was that Darcy was also forbidden to have anything to do with Wairaka, and when she arrived in the camp, she was captured and held prisoner.

"But you did, you did save Wairaka," the voice said, rubbing his arm. He turned to look at his aunty, saddened that Wairaka wasn't with him. But instead of seeing his aunty before him stood his little sister with Darcy right behind her.

He strained to see if it really was Wairaka through his tears. There she was standing right there.

"Is that really you? Are you really here?" he asked.

He stumbled backward, not believing that she was there. For a moment he thought that she may have been a ghost.

"You did save me," she said, holding her hand out to her big brother. "Thank you."

He held her badly bruised and battered face in his hands, gently kissing her forehead. He vowed that he would never again let any harm come to her.

That night they all sat around the fire in Whaea Panias whare. Kat and Te Miringa heard that during all of the commotion with Aramis and the haunting whale sounds, Parahi and Te Whao had rescued Darcy and he led them to Wairaka. At the same time, Matenga had taken advantage of the soldiers running from the tent and was there freeing her. They all headed back to the whare with Matenga going straight back to Kaiahi and Aramis. Having lived in the forest all of their lives and never heard such a ruckus, they knew that those sounds must've come from Aramis.

The sounds had shaken the camp to its very core, and the spooky lights in the forest had topped it off. The soldiers were hysterical, and by the time they had calmed down, Wairaka was gone.

Tamainupo, the chief, had joined them and had announced that the following day that there would be a feast in honor of Wairaka returning and welcoming Darcy into their family.

"That means that he is hers and she is his," Te Miringa said to Kat, smiling.

"Ohhhhhh, it's a wedding, wow!"

Tamainupō also thanked Aramis and Kat, knowing that without them, they would have never been able to get Wairaka back. Te

Huirama, Kokako, and other families arrived to what they thought would be a battle to save Wairaka. But instead was a celebration.

Aramis and Kat sat listening to tales beside the warm fire, tales of Huingariri entrusting the stone to Te Houpapa who entrusted it to Wharehuia, who entrusted it to Hinemoa and generations after until it came to Pania. They listened until their eyes could no longer stay open and they fell into a deep sleep.

CHAPTER SIXTEEN

"Wake up, sleepyhead, half of the day is wasted," a voice said.

Aramis slowly opened his eyes. Something was tickling his nose. As he looked down, he saw a mass of reddish orangey feathers. The same colour that he saw in the forest when they first arrived.

"It's Kaiahi's cloak. You must've really impressed him because he doesn't let anyone touch that. It has been passed down from generation to generation, to the highest warrior," Te Miringa said.

"Where's Kat?" Aramis asked, picking up the cloak to give back to Kaiahi. He felt very honored to have had that put over him while he slept.

"She's talking with Whaea Pania. It's nearly time for the ceremony"

Aramis walked out to be greeted by Kaiahi who introduced him to his entire family as the one that haunted the pākeha allowing Wairaka and Darcy to escape.

The sun was streaming down upon them warming their backs as if the sky had joined them to celebrate. Aramis was guided through the crowds by Kaiahi and introduced to a lot of different people. Everyone had gathered to witness the joining of Wairaka and Darcy. Everyone wore smiles. The females adorned their heads with circles of leaves. And the birds joined in singing beautiful melodies.

Then it was time. Aramis still hadn't found Kat. The ceremony started with some of the family performing a Pōwhiri, dancing in joy for the union that was about to take place. They twirled and sang and amongst them, he saw Whaea Pania and Te Miringa. Then he saw his little (in size, not age) sister. He was so proud of her at that moment. Then Darcy was officially welcomed into the family. He and Wairaka joined to become husband and wife. Darcy placed a beautiful iridescent black blue Korowai on Wairaka's shoulders and her eyes filled with tears. Tamainupō blessed the couple. They pressed their foreheads to each others nose sealing the union with a hongi. And then everyone cheered.

A special day indeed.

Celebration followed as everyone mingled. Aramis finally found Kat and swooped her into a big hug. "That was amazing," she squealed.

Gifts of food and precious Pounamu were given. Wairaka and Darcy kissed and thanked the twins and Wairaka gave Aramis the whale bone Taiaha for saving her life. Then Matenga stepped forward and handed Aramis his horn of shell. He pressed his forehead to Aramis and then said, "It's not often that I am wrong about a person, but maybe, this time, I may have been a little wrong," he said, smiling.

Aramis was overwhelmed, and for once in his life, lost for words.

"It's not very often that he's lost for words," Kat said, laughing. "We better leave," she said.

"Wait, you didn't think that you could just leave without this," Kaiahi said, handing his cloak to Aramis. Te Miringa gasped and everyone just stared.

"This was given to me with great honor, and now I pass it to you with great honor,"

Kaiahi said, putting the cloak around Aramis. Kat could've sworn that she saw Aramis eyes starting to well up.

The twins turned and walked into the dense forest. Aramis' eyes were filled with tears as Kat looked at him, smiling.

"You did good," she said, nudging him. "You really did."

Ancient Māori folklore tells of two spirits that were sent from the stars to protect the Māori in their time of need. The spirits sung a song that was so haunting that it scared the enemy away. They had appeared in the forest in a sea of mist and disappeared the same way after saving the chief's daughter and her husband. The Māori gave gifts of a sacred cloak made of red feathers, a horn of shell, a sacred whalebone Taiaha, and a carved box containing a stone of the sky. It is said that from time to time, when the mist rises in the forests, spirits are there, and to this day, they can still be heard in the forest singing their haunting songs of protection.

PART FOUR

MACEDONIA
311 BC

CHAPTER SEVENTEEN

On one of the brightest nights of the time, the stars all seemed to come out together to celebrate as a beautiful baby girl was born. Her parents, Tana and Aegeus, named her Eirini which meant Peace.

As Eirini grew, her mother Tana knew that her daughter, like herself and her mother before her, was gifted and could see events before they happened. Tana, whose name meant fire of the star goddess, also knew that within time, because of her gift, Eirini would be taken from them and sent to the temple to be raised as a priestess.

Having escaped this life herself, Tana wanted more for her daughter, and as the time grew nearer, Tana explained to Eirini what was expected and the serving of the oracle. She also told Eirini that she had other options, for Eirini to lead her own life and to experience love like she had.

Eirini, however, had decided on yet another path. She wanted to learn everything she could about the world. She wanted to travel. She wanted to experience far-off lands and cultures. She dreamed of learning literature, medicine and even philosophy. Even at a young age, Eirini had no intention of becoming a wife or a priestess.

She knew that to have the life she wished, she should have been a boy. She wished for a life free of the gods. She wished for a life of science and learning. Her father was so strong and handsome and he loved her and her mother with such intensity that it always took her breath away.

Her mother was flawlessly beautiful and had been a priestess for the oracle in the temple of the star. She would tell Eirini the story of how her father had come to the temple seeking guidance and left with a wife, and then she would always laugh with such love in her eyes.

One day, Eirini's father called her. "Where are you? Come here, my girl."

"Why are you dressed like that, Father?" Eirini asked, looking up at him.

Her father swept her up in his arms. He was dressed in a red tunic with a smaller white tunic over top of it. The military had come to their village and her father, like most able men in the village, had been made to join.

"Eirini," he said, "I need to go away."

"What? What do you mean?" she said in her five-year-old voice. Crouching down, her father looked straight into her big beautiful eyes and said, "Listen to me. I need to go away and you have to stay with your mother. Look after her, my beautiful girl. Tell her your stories and make her smile. Remember me every night before you go to sleep."

Her father, with his eyes filled with tears, hugged Eirini so tight that she thought he would squeeze the life out of her. Eirini, like her mother, knew that she would never see the father she knew again.

She watched as he walked toward the door of their home. She ran in front of the door, putting her arms out to try and stop him from leaving. She needed to tell him not to go.

Her mother sat sobbing with her head in her hands. Aegeus bent down to hug his daughter one final time, and she held onto him, begging him not to go. She knew what lay ahead of him. Aegeus's name meant protector and he fiercely protected them.

"Please don't go," she sobbed.

But both Tana and Aegeus knew that he had to. There was no choice. If he didn't go, the gods would be angered and a sacrifice would have to be made. A sacrifice of Tana and Eirini.

As her father went to leave, Eirini screamed, "NO! I won't let you go. I need you. We need you. Why are you going to fight for some king?" she shrieked angrily. "Tell him to go and do it himself, and maybe if he wasn't so lazy, he wouldn't be so fat," she said, stomping her foot on the ground with her fists clenched glaring at her father. Aegeus smiled at his defiant little girl.

"Never lose this," he whispered to her with a huge grin on his face. "Always lead yourself, Eirini. You have the whole world before you."

He turned and walked out the door.

CHAPTER EIGHTEEN

"Aeneas, wake up."

"What? What's wrong?"

"You were dreaming again, calling out about some fat lazy king."

"Really?" Aeneas grinned. "Maybe it wasn't a fat lazy king. Maybe I was calling out to you to get your fat lazy foot off my leg," he laughed.

Sitting up around the fire, Aeneas warmed himself.

"Here then, now that you're up, eat this," Egan said, thrusting bread in Aeneas' hands. "We move out soon," he said, looking toward the other troops. Maybe the Gods will be kind to us today and give us good weather to travel with."

Great, Aeneas thought to himself. *Another day trudging along another dusty road listening to more stories of heroes and gods that don't exist.*

Aeneas had learnt that to keep safe, he needed to keep his thoughts to himself and that also included never letting anyone know of his life before the military. He never told anyone where he was from and he never spoke of his life before he joined. All anyone knew was that he was fifteen, and he, along with Egan, were apprentices of Barak. Barak had acquired Aeneas when he was seven. He was an orphan and Barak found him alone as he passed through a desolate village that had been ravaged by war.

The Macedonian army was a strong and proud army, with thousands of soldiers made up from lands that they had conquered or passed through. This was how Barak came to be incorporated in the army. The army had travelled to Persia and Barak, already a well-known man of medicine and literature, was "asked" to join them. It was the kind of "ask" that you never refused.

Barak was a well-respected man. He was a man of the stars, a man of science, and would navigate the army. He was Persian and took a Greek name, which he thought was easier to pronounce.

Aeneas enjoyed learning how to navigate using the stars and Barak treated both Egan and himself as if they were his sons. He taught them about medicines and literature, science, and the universe.

And Barak, now and then on long journeys to pass the time, would tell of old prophecies, and in particular, he loved the prophecy about an angel and a star.

Aeneas was not at all interested in anything to do with beliefs or angels or gods. Barak, on the other hand, tried to fill the boys' minds with tolerance especially as the army they travelled with, adopted beliefs and customs of lands that they had conquered.

Aeneas would pretend to be listening and had become quite an expert of sleeping with his eyes open. On occasion, less than he would actually prefer, he did try to listen and believe. He really did but something inside his heart wouldn't allow him to believe in anything. His heart had been locked away a long time ago.

Life on the road serving the army was all that Aeneas knew, but his mind would sometimes wind back to when his heart was filled with love and happiness, back before the war that struck his village.

Something is coming, Aeneas thought to himself as he stared into the flames of the campfire that early morning. The flames were burning a bright orangey red. He was staring at the flames so intensely he forgot to blink and the heat from the fire started to make his eyes water. He had the same feeling he had the night before the army ravaged his village. Some sort of a sinking sad feeling in the pit of his stomach—fear and depression and utter helplessness. That awful feeling of being powerless.

"Where are we going?" Aeneas asked, as he looked up from the fire to where Egan was loading the wagon. "Feel free to help," he said to Aeneas.

Aeneas stood up from the fire with such a look of dread on his face that Egan dropped what he was carrying.

"What is it?" he asked Aeneas. "Was it the bread? I'm sorry, I only sat on it once."

"It's nothing. It must be something I ate other than that bread," he said as he punched Egan in the shoulder. He helped Egan load the wagon, but he had an uneasy feeling for the rest of the day. He was on edge and kept checking where the swords were in the wagon.

As the army travelled throughout the day and nothing eventuated, Aeneas started to relax and even managed a joke or two as they made camp that night. Aeneas put his anxiousness down to the recurring nightmares he had been having of a girl that was crying out for her father not to leave. The dreams haunted him night after night after night.

As Aeneas settled down for the night, he still kept a sword close by. He didn't know why. He was surrounded by thousands of armed quick-witted soldiers, but he felt that it may be required. Lying beside the crackling fire, he watched as the smoke danced up from the flames, dancing into the clear night sky. Looking up at the stars, unable to sleep, he felt as if someone was creeping behind him. He looked to either side of him.

"No, it's just his imagination. Barak and Egan are fast asleep" he muttered to himself. *Just close your eyes, Aeneas. Just close your eyes.* He closed his eyes and squeezed them shut. But Aeneas knew all too well that there was someone or something behind him. He could just sense it.

He opened his eyes and slowly, and ran his hand along the side of his body to where he knew the sword was. He grasped the sword.

Right, he thought. *Now what?*

He moved his head slowly away from the fire and turned towards the wagon. He saw two shadowy figures creeping along the side of it. He quietly looked over to Barak and Egan who were still asleep next to the fire. He could hear the two strangers whispering as they were attempting to steal from the wagon.

Crawling slowly from where he had slept, as if he were a lion stalking his prey, he stalked toward the wagon. In that very moment, he decided that he would not allow Barak and Egan to die. He looked back at Barak and Egan and found the courage to confront the strangers.

"I can do this. I can do this! For the people I love!" he whispered.

The crackling of the fire was so loud against the stillness of the night. He felt a lump in his throat and his heart started beating faster and faster. He held the sword tightly and noticed his hands shaking.

"Come on, Aeneas, you need to be a man. You need to protect them," he said, trying to encourage himself to stand up and confront the two strangers. He tried to muster all of his courage. He breathed hard and jumped up with his sword pointing straight at the throat of one of them.

"Bloody hell, you need to be careful with that, mate. You can poke an eye out," the voice said.

"Who are you?" Aeneas said, still standing with the sword pointing at them. Although Aeneas was shaking, they weren't about to argue with a person with a sword.

"Well," a small calm voice said, "I'm Kat, pleased to meet you." She held her hand out to Aeneas to shake his. Aeneas turned to face her with his sword that brushed up against Kat's top.

"You better back the hell away from my sister, bro," a strong, determined, protective voice said.

"This is my brother Aramis," Kat said. "It's okay, we're not here to hurt you," she said in her calming voice.

"Put that sword down before you hurt someone," Aramis demanded with an authoritative tone.

"Aramis, leave him. He's scared."

"I'm not scared," Aeneas said, trying not to speak with a shaky voice.

"Well, really? Then why are you shaking like you've had an electric shock, pal?" Aramis said, moving in closer to Aeneas.

"Leave him alone, Aramis," Kat said walking towards Aeneas. "It's okay," she said, reassuring Aeneas. "We're just looking for something. Maybe you've seen it. It's a piece of a crystal, kind of like this but maybe bigger." Kat held out her necklace so Aeneas could have a closer look at it.

Even in the stillness of the night, Kat could see Aeneas's reaction.

"You've seen it, haven't you? I can tell by the look on your face. Can you lead us to it? Kat asked Aeneas.

"Noooooo," he said, backing away, shaking his head. "Who are you?" he asked.

Kat and Aramis both looked at each other. "What's wrong?" Kat asked as she slowly walked toward Aeneas. Aeneas had tears running down his face.

"What's your name?" Kat asked. Aramis stood beside Kat, looking extremely uncomfortable that a boy was sobbing incessantly.

"Aeneas," he said with his head down. "My name is Aeneas."

"Aeneas. That's a cool name. Aeneas, do you know where the crystal is?"

Aeneas shook his head "No. I don't"

"Urrgggghhhh, we're going around in circles," Aramis complained turning towards his sister. "Clearly, he doesn't know."

"But he does know," Kat said, looking at Aeneas. "I can tell he knows."

"No, I don't. I don't know where it is now!"

"Now? What do you mean now? Have you seen it before?" Aramis, trying to be as diplomatic as he could, tried to probe for information.

"Yes, I have. My mother had one just like that."

"Cool, okay, now we're talking. So just tell us where your mum is and we'll go and see her," Aramis said, looking at Aeneas.

"You can't."

"We can't?"

"No, you can't."

"Why can't we?"

"Because ... because she's dead," Aramis said, shaking, looking down at the ground.

"Oh," Kat said in a hushed tone "I'm so sorry to hear that,"

"How did she die?" Aramis said sheepishly, now regretting his thoughts of Aeneas.

"She was killed when the army went through. They killed her and burnt the village. Barak—that's him over there—he saved me. He stopped and picked me up."

"Hold on. You are with the army that killed your mother?" Aramis asked, looking at Kat.

"Stop judging," Kat said. "You have to do what you have to do."

"Not judging—nope, not judging at all. Just, y'know, they killed his mother."

"It was a long time ago. I was seven then. Now I'm fifteen, and I've been with Barak and Egan since then," he said, turning to look at them again.

"I don't understand," Aramis said to Kat. "The map brought us here so it must be here. Someone in the army here must have it."

"Someone has her necklace?"

"Yes, sorry about that. Someone does. This crystal glows when another crystal other than my brother's is near, and it's glowing right now."

"So does that mean that my mother's murderer is here?"

"Well, maybe, I'm not sure about that one, but the crystal is definitely here."

Aeneas's face changed from disbelief and shock to anger. He stopped crying and was no longer shaking. "The murderer has been with me all along. I've travelled with the person that took my mother's life. I had assumed that ... that soldier had perished along with her."

"But," Aramis said, "if your mother had the crystal, then she would've been protected. She couldn't have been hurt unless the person was known to her or the crystal was stolen from her."

Aeneas looked puzzled.

"What can you remember about that day, Aeneas?"

"I can't really remember much. It was such a long time ago. I remember my mother saying that she had happy news. There were fresh flowers in the house and she was happy. Really happy like when my father was with us. He left with an army years before. She was happy like that when they were together. She was singing and it was like father was back with us."

"Did she say who was coming?"

"No, she just told me to run and put on my best dress and that the big surprise will be here soon."

"Wait ... dress?" Aramis said. Aeneas looked shocked but Aramis continued on "Did you just say 'dress'? So you're a chick, not a dude?"

"Chick? Ummm, no, I'm a person. What is this dude you speak of?"

"Y'know, dude, bloke."

Kat explained for Aramis "Male. He means you're a female, not a male. You're a girl?"

Aeneas sighed. A secret he - she had carried for so long finally said aloud "Yes, I'm actually a girl."

"Then why are you pretending to be a boy?" Aramis asked, trying to push the sword away from himself.

"Do not touch me again," Aeneas said, holding the sword to Aramis's throat.

"Woah, dude, what the hell! You seriously need to put a lid on that attitude you have going on."

"I told you I am not a dude," Aeneas snarled back.

"Dude, bloke, bro, chick, whatevs—you're the girl pretending to be a boy who's wearing a dress and sandals soooo ... ," Aramis said, shrugging his shoulders toward Aeneas.

"I don't like you," she said with quiet menace to Aramis.

"Sweet as," he said back. "I'm not exactly warming to you either, bro."

CHAPTER NINETEEN

Aeneas reluctantly started to tell the twins her story of how she thought her mother had died at the hand of the army. Aeneas had seen it in her mind just moments before it happened and ran home to warn her mother but was too late.

Travelling with the army was Barak. He took pity on Eirini who was now orphaned as he passed through and took her with him, telling her that a life on the road was no place for a girl. He gave the seven-year-old a choice, to travel with him as his apprentice or stay with her dead mother and die as well.

Although Eirini was scared, even at such a young age she knew what she had to do. She chose to leave with Barak. Barak told her that she would need to become a boy to stay safe, and he cut off her hair and changed her name to Aeneas, a famous warrior of the past.

As Eirini left her village with Barak, she looked back at the smoldering village with clouds of smoke wafting up through the air, her heart breaking with the loss of her mother and all that she loved. The loss of the life she had known as Erini. She knew that she needed to harden herself and step into the life of Aeneas. And with that her knowing, her seer abilities had disappeared.

"Sorry, mate," Aramis said, nudging Aeneas. "I didn't know." Aeneas, holding her sword, glared at Aramis.

"Okay, okay," Holding up his hands "I'm backing up now. Geez," he said.

Kat stood in between Aeneas and Aramis. "So what would you like us to call you, Eirini or Aeneas?" she asked.

"I've been Aeneas for such a long time, well, I like Aeneas," she said, nodding to Kat. "I would like to find out who killed my mother, so I will help you search for the crystal."

Aeneas stood shoulders back with a fixed glare around the camp. "I will make you pay for taking my mother's life" she said under her breath.

"Alrighty then." Aramis clenched his teeth and motioned to Kat. "We can't take her with us to find the crystal. She's one sandwich short of a picnic. What if she nuts out on us and loses it? We'll never find the crystal."

"I think we should give her a chance," Kat said, "If she starts to go rogue, we can rein her back in."

"Ha, you can rein her back in. She's out there, wayyyyy out there like a galaxy out there."

"Oh stop being a drama queen," Kat teased Aramis.

The three crept through the camp following the light of the crystal. The crystal started glowing brighter and brighter. "It must be near," Kat whispered.

"What's over there?" she said to Aeneas.

"That's the generals' tent," she answered. "Why? Is the crystal near his tent?"

"Well, the crystal is pointing that way so it must be near there."

"Are you crazy? The General is ruthless. We can't go there! He has had soldiers killed for just looking at him. I have never ever seen him. He's just come here from leading one of Alexander's larger armies and he never lost a battle. He's been made one of Alexander's companions. It's a great honor, but the talk in the camp was that he's cruel, a cruel, heartless man. He had his family murdered so he could continue to go to war and had them replaced by marrying Alexander's cousin."

"Oh, fantastic! Just the kinda person we need to know—not!" Aramis said, looking at Kat. The three crept closer toward the tent.

"Stop, you three, what are you doing here?" a voice commanded.

Thinking fast Kat replied "Oh, we are just taking the general's medicine,"

"Medicine? What medicine?" the guard asked.

"It's not something that we should really talk about, y'know, it's private."

"Let me check," the guard said, turning to leave to ask about the medicine.

"Check this!" Aramis said as he hit the guard over the head with a pot. There was only one guard so Aeneas thought that must've meant that the general was asleep. They slowly crept inside the tent. Aeneas went first and Kat and Aramis were right behind her in single file.

"Why have you stopped? Aeneas, get moving before we're ..."

CHAPTER TWENTY

"Well, well, well, is that you, little Eirini? I knew you hadn't died in the village. Always a defiant one."

Aeneas stood staring at the general, shaking like a leaf. She looked as if she had seen a ghost.

"Leave us," the general said to his guards that were inside his tent.

The three were face to face with the general who seemed to know Aeneas.

"What is it?" the general asked in a mocking, patronizing voice. "Come, Eirini, did you think I was dead? Like your poor sweet mother?" he scoffed. Aramis and Kat looked at Aeneas and the general.

"Well, speak, girl, say something. Who are your little friends?" the general asked while pouring himself a drink of wine.

The general's tent was covered in luxurious carpets. To the left was a large bed and to the right where he was standing was a table covered in brass urns and glasses. Huge candles on metal poles illuminated the red-walled tent that was fringed with gold tassels.

"Who is he?" Kat whispered to Aeneas.

"My father," Aeneas replied, trembling. "He's my father."

Kat and Aramis then realized that the big surprise must've been Aeneas' father coming home.

"I don't understand. You're alive? You know of Mother dying? Why didn't you come for me?" she asked.

"Have a seat," the general said to the three.

"Nah, we're all good here, thanks," replied Aramis.

"No, please, I really must insist" he drawled.

"Oh god, this isn't going to end well," Aramis said, looking for an emergency exit.

"Why didn't I come for you?" he mocked. "Hmmmm, let me think—oh yes ... I didn't come for you because I didn't want you" he laughed. "I never wanted you," Aeneas' face was twisted in anger and sadness. "Oh, Eirini, little Eirini. You were never meant to be. I only ever wanted this." Aegeus held Tana's necklace in front of Aeneas.

"Yes, Eirini, it was me. All those years ago. I sent word to your mother that I was coming home. She would never let me see the crystal. She always guarded it. I pretended to love her. I had to literally force myself every day to love her. You don't know what a relief it was when I was called back to the army. I could be my normal self instead of being stuck in a smothering, disgusting, needy relationship." Aeneas looked heartbroken. Her whole world shattered again.

"My army had been defeated, and I was about to lose them when I heard of this priestess who was a guardian of a piece of a star that was a crystal. And this crystal would protect whoever owned it. Alexander said that if I had the crystal that I would win battle after battle, and he would make me a general in charge of my own army and one of his companions. I went to the temple to meet her, your mother. Do you think that that was an accident?" He laughed again, sipping on his wine

"It was planned. I was to go to the temple and steal the crystal, but Tana was on guard. She didn't trust me, so then I decided that I had to gain her trust. I visited her every day for months until she finally started to trust me. I came so close to getting this damn necklace, but then we were interrupted by the oracle. The only way that I could get the crystal was to get your mother away from the temple. So I played along and told her I loved her. She fell for it hook, line, and sinker," he cackled with a big smirk spread across his face.

"And she agreed to marry me. I thought that that would be it. I would have access to the crystal and I would leave, but Tana had other ideas. She hid the necklace, and no matter what I tried to do, she wouldn't show me it. You see, the only way that I was going to become a general was if I had the crystal. Alexander didn't trust me, but once I had the crystal, he would give me everything I had ever wanted. If only she had given me the crystal she could still be alive today. But it turns out that she was more defiant than you," he said, smirking.

"I had lost a few battles and Alexander was looking to replace me. I knew that the only thing that would be able to save me was this crystal. I convinced him to give me one more chance. So I sent word to your mother that I was to return. Your mother was so happy to see me." He laughed.

"She forgot that she was wearing her necklace. I asked her to hand it to me and she refused. So I took it from her and left. I ordered one of my guards to kill her. I didn't need her anymore. I was engaged to Alexander's cousin, but the guard was weak and couldn't do it. He couldn't kill an ex-priestess. Me, on the other hand, I didn't have a problem. So I did it. I killed your mother. And then the guard. And now you're here to take back the crystal? You and your little friends? I don't think so, girl! This is mine!"

His words were filled with such hatred and venom that Aeneas couldn't bear to listen to anymore.

"Stop it! Stop, stop! You're my father. How can you say all this? You loved us. I know you did!" she pleaded, sobbing, her heart breaking with what she had just heard.

"Yes, Eirini, I am your father, but no, I never loved you or your mother. I did what I had to do to get what I wanted and now I have it. No one has been able to stop me since." He laughed. "I am invincible."

Aeneas flew into a fit of rage and charged Aegeus with her sword tightly clenched in her hand, screaming, "MURDERERRRRRR!"

He fell to the ground on his knees, blood soaking through his shirt. A look of utter confusion spread across his bright red face "But ... but I have the crystal," he said, looking at his hand.

"Looking for this?" Aramis said, holding the crystal out in front of him. "It's all about misdirection, mate, misdirection!"

Aeneas stood staring at the man she knew as her father. He fell forward onto his face with a sword thrusted in his back. She was shaking so much that she didn't realize that her sword was still in her hands.

"Quickly," a voice whispered from behind them. Aeneas was still standing in front of her father in shock.

"We've got to go, Aeneas. We need to go now," Aramis said, grabbing her arm. She stumbled out of the tent, with a haze of emotions flooding through her body. Everything that she thought she knew was a lie. Pain and grief surged through her. She wanted to run, run and run far away. Run away where no one could ever find her. She couldn't stop sobbing.

"Aeneas, Aegeus will be discovered soon. It's not safe for you now. You need to leave here. The guards have seen you and your friends."

"Barak? Is that you?" she asked doubled over, ready to vomit. "Yes, it's me. Now hurry! You need to leave."

"Come with us," Aramis said to Aeneas. "You'll be safe."

"Can you and Egan come?" Aeneas asked Barak.

"No, Aeneas, our place is here, but yours is to go with your friends. I knew this from the moment I saw you," Barak told Aeneas as they hurried back toward the wagons. They heard the sounds of guards running toward Aegeus's tent.

"But where are your horses?" Barak asked Kat.

"Oh no, we have a different way of travelling," she said, smiling.

Barak looked at Aeneas and said, "Take this" he handed Aeneas a leather-bound book with a Merkaba on the front surrounded by constellations. The hair on the back of Kat's neck stood up. It was the book of peace, the book that Lu had.

"Wow, is this your book? Did you write it?" Kat asked Barak.

"No, it is beautiful, but I am not blessed with the patience and the know-how to create this. A traveler had come to me when I had just started medicine. I was twenty-two, I believe. He was ill and in exchange for help, he gave me this beautiful book."

Kat opened the book and inside was a complete map. It looked as if it was written yesterday.

"Who was the man? Did he tell you his name?" Kat asked.

"No, he was a seerer though. He said that one day I would raise two strong boys and that one would marry and provide me with many grandchildren and that the other would leave to travel and to give this book to her travel companions. He said 'her' and I said, 'Don't you mean *his*?' The seer just smiled and left. I remember he spoke with a strange accent, much like yours, but then he was a traveler after all. I just thought he was drowsy from the medicine I had given him. That was almost thirty years ago."

"Someone gave Barak this book knowing years ago that we would be coming here and to give us the book? That doesn't make sense. Who are these people?" Kat said.

"Nothing bloody well makes sense," Aramis mumbled back, studying the map.

"Look, AD is written on the map in the part that we never had. Soooo that must mean 'after death'?" she said. "But then there's 'dkm' over here. Goodness knows what that means. So over here on Lu's map was where the pencil markings were, but they're not here. They must've been written later?"

Aramis and Kat looked at each other.

Aeneas hugged Barak so tight. She never wanted to let him go. He kissed her on her head.

"Go, my boy, and be the best girl that you can be," he whispered to her smiling, "and may the light of the stars guide and protect you all."

Aramis took her hand and said, "It's getting light. We need to go."

"Say goodbye to Egan and tell him he's the best big brother anyone could have ever asked for, and Barak," she said, "I will always love you. You are my father, and I will remember you every night before I sleep."

"And I you, my girl. I will look for you in the stars."

Aramis looked at Aeneas and said, "Hold my hand and remember to breathe" as Kat held the map with Tana's crystal over it.

A flash of brilliant lights swirled in front of them, forming a tunnel. Flashes of lightning and stars swished around the inside of the tunnel like a whirlwind. Aeneas looked back at Barak for one last time and walked into the tunnel with the twins.

PART FIVE

INDIA
1278

CHAPTER TWENTY-ONE

"Okay, guys, when are we?" Aramis said, looking around. Dirt. Dry dirt was all they could see for miles.

Kat was looking at the map in the book that Barak gave Aeneas, and Aeneas was, well, Aeneas was standing in the corner up against a huge rock vomiting everywhere.

"Yep, it'll get you, but that's just in the beginning. You'll get used to it," Aramis said, looking at Aeneas.

"Sit down," he said. Aeneas was trying to find something to hold onto. "Until your head stops ..." Aeneas was pointing at her head.

"Yep, until it stops spinning," said Kat.

"It's dry and dusty and the map looks like it's India, but I'm not sure where in India. If it's dry then that should be central because the south is tropical and the north is colder."

"It's just dry dirt and dry dirt and more dry dirt," Aramis said, looking around at the bleak landscape.

"Okay, so if I can see a fort made of rock or stone? A bloody big fort ... ,"Aramis said, looking into the distance.

"Then central I'd say," Kat replied, still looking at the book of peace that Barak gave them.

Aeneas, thinking she was fully recovered, stood up. Her head wooshed and whirled. Still wobbly, she decided to quickly sit back down again.

"So we're in India." Kat flicked through the BOP (Book of Peace) as Aramis fondly named it.

Aeneas couldn't make sense of anything. India? What on earth?

"Anything about India?" he said, looking over Kat's shoulder at the BOP. "There's nothing there," he exclaimed in a high-pitch squeal sounding like a balloon being deflated. "The page is empty. What's the point of that? I hope the whole book isn't like that."

"Hold on," Kat took her crystal off and held it over a blank page. The page slowly started coming alive. It was amazing, like watching an ancient drawing pop into 3D. A hologram appeared. The fort began to rise up off the page. The ginormous stone walls around the fort appeared, and then another larger and higher stone wall snaked its way around the inner fort. The map showed a caravan of camels nearing it. The caravan of at least a hundred camels looked as if they were inside a golden bubble, glowing a brilliant bright golden glow. All of the camels were covered in heavily embroidered cloth and carried bags and jeweled studded trunks laden with treasures.

The bags and boxes were also studded with jewels that sparkled like stars dancing across the bright night sky. The book showed the caravan slowly winding through the desert toward the fort and then a child from the fort leading the caravan inside to a watering hole.

The three watched as they saw the child sneak back to the caravan while everyone was resting. The child took something from a bag that was on one of the camels and ran into the inner fort, and then the book showed the caravan later continuing on their journey. However the caravan was no longer travelling inside a gold bubble and surrounded by a bright light. The bright light was now over the fort.

"Ohhhhh, great, so how exactly are we supposed to get into a fort to find a thief?" Aramis said, worriedly looking at the book. "I suppose I could use my handsomeness and charm my way in," he said with a wink, thinking out loud.

"We want to get into the fort," Aeneas said, trying to stand up "not thrown out!"

"Hahahaha! So not funny," replied Aramis with his usual sarcastic tone

"I don't know," Kat said, answering Aramis' original question, "but that's where the crystal is - so that is where we have to go"

"I know," Aeneas blurted out in a hurry to contribute to the conversation. "Why don't we follow a caravan in. This area looks desolate so a caravan will need to stop and rest before carrying on to the next location. Just a thought but it may work."

Aramis and Kat looked around and all they could see for miles was dry, barren, dusty land, desert lands—nothing as far as the eye could see apart from sand and a few scraggly trees.

"Well, we don't have any other plan," Kat said, shrugging her shoulders.

Aramis put his hand up as if to suggest another plan.

"Serious plans. We don't have any other serious plans. So let's give this a go," Kat said, looking at her brother as he put his hand down.

CHAPTER TWENTY-TWO

The three walked toward the fort. They could hear the hustle and bustle of people inside the walls. The inner fort was perched high on a hill with huge stone walls, encircling it like a snake coiled and ready to strike. Honey-coloured stone walls jutted out either side of the fort that looked like giant snakes crawling along the ridgeline, in opposite directions.

As the three neared the outer walls of the fort, a small caravan of eight camels appeared. The caravan, although small, was brightly coloured. The camels wore beautiful harnesses covered in large tassels of brightly coloured wool that made them look stunningly regal. On the harnesses were also tassels with small metal bells. They gently rang with each gliding step that the majestic camels took. And to top it off, draped around each of the camel's necks were what could only be described as necklaces of woven multicoloured braids of thread covered in sparkling beads of glass and more bells. Each camel had at least five of these necklaces running down their long slender neck. There were also woven braids that were covered in glittering glass beads around their legs and hooves. They were magical.

Aramis and Kat thought Aeneas was going to cry from shock upon seeing camels for the first time in her life. Imagine for a moment a flying carpet, a beautiful intricately woven magnificent flying magical carpet, then imagine a huge heavily embroidered tented canopy of clashing bright jewel colours draping over a bed with exquisitely carved posts holding up that canopy. Then imagine that magical carpet and exquisite tented canopy bed sitting on top of a majestic camel. Imagine all of that, the sheer beauty and awe as this giant animal gracefully glided toward you, because that was exactly what was walking toward Aeneas, Aramis, and Kat.

Aeneas looked as though she was going to pass out from either shock or excitement. Her facial expressions were hard to gauge at that very moment. She just stood there with her mouth wide open, pointing at the camels.

They were, without a doubt, the most spectacular thing that Aeneas had ever laid her eyes on. The camels' faces looked as if they were wearing makeup as they seemed to bat their luscious long eyelashes at Aramis, which made him a little nervous. The three asked if they could help the owner water their camels in return for any pieces of clothing that they may have spare. Aramis and Kat had learned that to blend in. Hoodies and jeans stuck out like a sore thumb, and Aeneas was dressed like a Macedonian soldier wearing a short tunic.

The owner of the caravan was a merchant called Devdash. He agreed as the three said that they knew their way around the fort and could help him find somewhere to rest for the evening.

"That sounds great," Devdash said, smiling. However, as he inspected all three, he thought that it may be easier to give the clothing now to avoid any unwanted attention. "Is this how you dress here in this place? Your clothing is very peculiar," he said, looking at the three.

Aeneas started to speak and quietly said, "Yes, well, we were—"

"Robbed," Aramis said, jumping in.

"Yes, robbed, yes, that's right," Kat said, nodding her head.

Thankfully Devdash believed the lie.

CHAPTER TWENTY-THREE

The three walked into the fort with the caravan, thinking that they had a general idea of where the watering hole was from the book. They were in for a huge surprise upon passing through the enormous gates of the fort.

They soon realized that looking at a map and looking at the same location in real life was completely different. Once inside the fort walls, they were immediately hit by a kaleidoscope of chaotic colours. The hustle and bustle of a busy bazaar had stalls not only perched up against the honey-coloured stone walls of the outer fort, but there were stalls everywhere lining the streets, in the middle of street, and some just looked like the vendor couldn't find a spot so they just stopped and set up shop right there in the middle of everything.

The walls were at least six stories high, with six-to-seven-storied buildings that looked like pierced jewel boxes plonked on top of each other, with random verandas thrown in for good luck.

There were vendors everywhere selling everything a traveler may need. Ladies dressed in clashing colours of bright silks that swept over their bodies and faces. Everywhere you turned, you were met with a cacophony of noise, colours, and smells that was absolutely intoxicating.

Scents of sweet treats and heavenly dishes wormed their way through the market, enticing the weary traveler to part with their hard-earned gold. The streets were so crowded that you could barely move. The three tried to maneuver the camels through the endless twisting and turning of streets and bamboozling alleyways.

"Are you sure you know where you're going? My camels are tired and that rumbling you heard wasn't the ground. It was my stomach," he said, smacking his hand against it.

"Ummm yeah sure, of course we know where we're going," Aramis said out of the corner of his mouth, having absolutely no idea of where they were going. He looked at Kat hoping she would have an idea but she was just as stumped.

They meandered through the bazaar, around and around in circles until Devdash gave up and said, laughing, "So, you're from around here are you?" He had a huge grin on his face. "Come with me," he said, "You three couldn't lead yourself out of this place, let alone lead us to water. Look, there's a sign over there, and we have passed it four times already." He laughed, pointing to a huge sign saying, "Water." He took the camel leads off the three.

"Sorry, what gave it away?" Kat asked.

"Well, I don't know. Maybe the clothing, the hair, the shoes, and the fact that you three look like you haven't eaten in weeks. This place is one of the wealthiest forts in the area. Everyone gets to eat here."

They followed Devdash as he watered the camels then he led them through some alleyways to rows of multi-leveled stone buildings, which looked like modern-day terraced homes with doors and shutters of all different shapes, sizes, and colours. The buildings were covered in vines of crimson and fuchsia coloured flowers and were just majestically gorgeous. Aramis, Aeneas and Kat just stood staring, trying to absorb everything.

CHAPTER TWENTY-FOUR

Devdash looked at his stomach and said, "I'm hungry." He paused at a door. "Shall I go and ask them for food?" he asked the three.

"Hmmm, noooo, this house doesn't look inviting." They walked on.

"What about this house?" he said, pausing again and looking at them as they stared blankly back at him.

"No? Okay, maybe farther on then," he said as they continued to walk for another five or ten minutes, pausing at several other homes while Devdash pondered whether or not to go and ask for food until they happened upon a turquoise-coloured carved door. The house was like the others made of stone but had intricate carvings of people that looked as if they were dancing along the top of the door and beautiful trellis laced the sides of the double doors.

He turned to the three and said, "I'm tired. This place looks as good as any," he said, shrugging his shoulders.

"Shall I just go in and see if they have any food? What do you think? I'm hungry, and if I left finding food to you three, we would all die of starvation," he said, smiling. "You three stay out here. I'll see if I can be like Aramis and see if my handsome looks can charm the owner. Okay."

The three all looked worried. Devdash was a lovely and gentle man but handsome was not a trait that he possessed. They watched as he put his ear to the door, and slowly opening it, he turned and looked at them with his finger pressed up against his lips, and then he crept inside.

"Is he breaking in? He didn't even knock. He just walked in. Oh my goodness, he's breaking in," Kat said, starting to panic.

"We have to stop him. They cut your hands off around here for stealing," Aramis said, equally panicking.

Just then they heard screaming and running and yelling. They heard what sounded like metal pots being thrown at someone and smashing against the hard stone floors. The three immediately ran through the door to stop Devdash from stealing food only to find him lying on the floor covered with what looked like a mountain of small children and a lady standing above him holding a large brass urn, laughing.

"Help me," he tried to say while reaching out to them.

The three look puzzled. Other than Devdash barely being visible under the swarm of tiny bodies, he didn't seem to be in any danger.

"What's going on?" Kat yelled to Devdash over the childrens' screams while helping him stand up.

"Get off me, you wretched children. I'm here to steal some food for my friends," he said.

"Hahhahahaha!" the children laughed and laughed. "You're so funny."

"Steal food?" the lady with the brass urn said. "You can steal whatever you want. You stole my heart years ago."

"Ewwwwww, that's disgusting," the children said as Devdash kissed the lady.

Devdash turned to Kat, Aramis and Aeneas with his arms outstretched. "Welcome to my home," he said laughing. "And meet my children." They swarmed around the three all at once. "I call them 1, 2, 3, 4, 5, 6, then yellow and green and blue and orange and crimson and pink." He laughed, pointing at various children.

"Stop it, Father," they laughed back. "Did you bring us a present?"

"Yes, present, present, present!" they were all shouting, bouncing up and down clapping their hands as if they had springs attached to their feet.

"Maybe I did, maybe I didn't," he joked, kissing and hugging them all.

"You're home?" Aeneas laughed. "Soooo all that time we spent walking around trying to find water ... was?"

"Was," Devdash said, "the most fun I have had in a very long time. You three pretending to know where you were going."

His wife hugged all three, "He says that you need food," she said, pointing to her husband. "I think he's right."

That night they dined like royalty in the hospitality of Devdash and his family. They sat listening as he told stories of his travels. His old camels would probably be able to make one more trip and then who knows what he will do.

"But," he said, "that is of no concern of yours. Tonight we enjoy ourselves and tomorrow we worry," he said, laughing.

The laughter of the twelve children, the smell of incense mixed with the scent of exotic spices, and the aromas of heavy perfumes hung in the air of the colour-saturated home. Devdash had also invited his three brothers and their families for dinner as well.

Aeneas had never experienced such beauty crammed into one tiny space. Nor had she experienced such hospitality especially from complete strangers. She was mesmerized and hung on every word they said. She was in complete heaven.

CHAPTER TWENTY-FIVE

As night slowly started to turn light, the three, not wanting to wake their hosts, quietly left Devdash and his wife Amira's home. As they walked out into the street, the sun still slowly climbing into the sky, the three searched for a way into the inner fort.

They were completely daunted but undeterred by the sheer undertaking of the task ahead.

"We've gotta get in there. There's no other way," Kat said.

"Okay, but how on earth are we going to get past them?" Aramis said, staring straight at the four guards who were standing in front of the inner fort wooden doors.

The doors must've been at least several stories high. Large enough to let two or three elephants with carriages on their backs pass seamlessly through. The doors were covered in huge metal spikes, and both Aeneas and Aramis wondered how they could ever be opened.

"I read somewhere that elephants have to pull them open," Kat said.

"Well, there must be an easier way in and out because they wouldn't have opened the gates for the thief, and the crystal is in there so they must've come in and out undetected."

The three all stood staring at the closed doors in complete awe of the sheer grandeur of them. They were huge and fortified but also beautiful. They had no idea how they would get this crystal.

"What are you three doing?" A voice whispered, giving them a big fright. To their relief it was Devdash. "You can't be here," he said, ushering them away from the main entrance.

The three were very happy to see their friend again. They told Devdash that they needed to get inside the inner fort.

"There's something of ours in there. Well, not really ours. It's a long story," Kat mumbled to a confused looking Devdash.

"Are you thieves?" he asked.

"No, not exactly, we're more like liberators," Aramis said.

"Liberators around here are what we call thieves," said Devdash, looking sternly at the three.

"Come home with me and tell me what's really going on. Amira and I will see what we can do to help."

As the three followed Devdash back home, they started to tell him about the star of peace and that one of the pieces was within the inner fort walls.

Devdash looked at them with that kind of look you have when you want to believe what you're hearing but at the same time you think that the person telling the story is slightly bonkers.

"I know it sounds like a load of rubbish," Aramis said "But it's actually true. We're travelers from somewhere else and we need to reunite all of the pieces of the star."

Devdash stood in front of them. "I think we're going to need some hot tea for this," he said as Amira entered the room.

For the next hour, the three tried to explain to Devdash and Amira about the star and their quest. She had a look of disbelief on her face. Devdash and Amira looked at each other as if to say, "We let these three stay in our house near our children?".

"Let me ask you, what do you intend to do with the star? Why do you need it?"

"It will save all of humanity. Once it's all together again, all of the pieces. It will save mankind" Kat explained

"We're not crazy," Aramis added, looking at their bewildered faces. Disbelief still showed on Devdash's face. Amira's too.

"Let me show you something," Kat said, pulling out the BOP while Aeneas told them the story of the caravan with a hundred camels in a bubble of gold light and then how a thief stole something and now the bubble of light is over the inner fort.

Kat turned to the map and asked Aeneas if she could have her mother's crystal. Aeneas took the crystal from around her neck.

"Please don't be scared" Aeneas said, "It's not trickery or magic. Well, it's kind of magic but it won't hurt you. It helps us locate the crystals."

As Kat held the crystal over the blank page in the book, Devdash and Amiras' eyes widened, as it started coming to life.

"What is it? Is it safe?" Amira asked, scared and fascinated at the same time. She reached out to touch the 3D holograms, her hand sweeping right through them. Devdash looked at her then back at the book. He equally seemed scared but, at the same time, curious, very curious.

To the astonishment of the three, the map no longer showed the caravan but the inner fort. It showed the thief removing bricks of stone from the outer fort wall then crawling through the small space. They saw the thief running through gardens and then briefly stopping to change clothes. Then they saw the thief calmly walking up some stairs and saw guards moving aside to let the thief into a room.

"That would mean that the thief is known to the guards. What is in that area?" Aeneas asked Devdash

"I think that's the ladies' court, where all the wives are. If the thief is in there, then the thief is either a royal wife or a servant" Devdash answered

"By the way the guards moved aside, I'd say that she is a wife," Amira said, still looking at the map.

Aramis was stumped. How on earth would they get inside? He turned to Devdash and asked if they knew anyone in the ladies court.

"Us? No, we're mere merchants. We're good merchants, but no, I can honestly say that it's impossible to get in," Devdash said, throwing his hands in the air. "Absolutely impossible."

"Unless ..."Amira said, looking at Devdash with an air of certainty.

"Unless?" Devdash asked, looking at Amira.

"Unless ... we find one of those hidden tunnels that lead to a passageway that your brother Davinder spoke about," Amira replied.

"Are you mad?" exclaimed Devdash, thumping his fist on the table. "Do you know what happens to people who are caught in the inner fort?"

"Yes, I do. Nothing happens because Davinder and your other two brothers are still alive," she said, sitting beside Devdash with a raised eyebrow.

"Oh please, they were just boys when they did that," said Devdash.

"Yes, they were, but they still did that, didn't they?" Amira said in a tone that signaled Devdash not to try her patience.

"Did what? What did they do?" asked Aeneas.

"Okay, all right." Devdash said with a sigh and began telling them a story from his childhood. The story of his brothers and the princess, "When I was very small, one of my three brothers fell in love. In love with a girl who was destined to marry the king".

Kat gasped. This story was going to be a good one for sure. Devdash went on to tell them of how his brother, Davinder - the one in love, had convinced Vijaye and Suneel, his two other brothers, to help her escape. All three of them thought they could do it. Legend of the secret tunnels and passageways is well known. But everyone believed it to be simply a story. Little did they know - the tunnels and passageways were true. And the brothers actually made it in. Made it into the fort and then into the ladies' court.

"No way! Oh my goodness, how did they do it?" Kat asked excitedly, perched on the edge of her seat.

"How did they do it, Amira?" Devdash said as he signaled to her wife to take over and tell the story of the brothers and the princess.

"Well," Amira began. The three listened so intently, so interested to see where the story went "With a little ingenuity and help from my sisters, they disguised themselves as ladies," she said with a laugh. Aramis' face was in complete shock. "Apparently, they were so convincing that one of the guards even asked Suneel out. They slipped into the ladies' court and eventually made their way to the princess only to find that she had no intention of leaving the palace. She was too fond of all the riches and had no intention of ever marrying Davinder. Heartbroken, Davinder and his brothers left the fort," Amira said.

"Heartbroken? He was dating your sister a week later." Devdash laughed.

"Yes, he certainly was and now they have been happily married for the past twenty years and have fourteen happy, beautiful children." she replied, smiling.

"So your brothers would know a way in?" Aramis asked Devdash.

"Maybe," Devdash said, looking worried.

"There's only one way to know," Amira said to Devdash "go and see them".

CHAPTER TWENTY-SIX

Devdash took the three to his brother's home who coincidentally happened to be the homes that they had stopped at when he was pretending to consider asking for food. Aramis had a big grin on his face.

"What? You didn't expect me to stop at a stranger's home for food," he said, laughing.

The three spoke with the brothers who laughed and joked about the memories and then decided to help, thinking how much fun it would be, as long as they, the three on their travels, told the story of their heroism.

"Heroism?" the brothers' wives said, each rolling their eyes and laughing.

It seemed that Devdash's entire family had the biggest sense of humor that the three had ever encountered. Their laughs were infectious and the brothers and their families lived every day as if it was a celebration of life. "And why not?" Vijaye would say. "Life is too short not to have fun."

They agreed to show the three the secret tunnels that had been there for hundreds of years, which most had forgotten. The brothers only found them when one of them fell into a hole that turned out to be a tunnel.

They waited until darkness crept its shadowy blanket upon the fort, and the four brothers led Aramis, Kat, and Aeneas through the twisting, winding tunnels that had been cut into the sandstone under the fort.

"I wonder what these tunnels were originally for?" Kat whispered.

"Maybe to smuggle out princesses," Suneel, walking before Kat, replied.

Their spirits high, they were still a little apprehensive with what lay ahead. As they reached the end of the tunnel, Vijaye told the three that they cannot go any further. They were men and would be spotted, but they would wait there in the tunnels for the three to return.

"What about Aramis? He's a male," Aeneas said.

"Yes, but he should be fine. With our big fat bodies and sore backs, we just can't make it through the opening in time."

Climbing out of the tunnel, Kat whispered the plan one more time, "The court is over that way. We head up those stairs and then turn to the left. The princess or bride-to-be—whoever she is—should be in the room straight opposite the hallway. We go in, get the crystal, and leave. Got it?"

"Got it. But what if she won't give it?" Aeneas said.

"Well, we'll cross that bridge when we get to it. Let's go."

The three ran across the grassy area and ran up the stairs. The air was cool and their hearts were beating so fast and hard they could have sworn that they could be heard by the entire fort. They turned left and ran straight into the princess's room.

"Hello," Kat said quietly, "is anyone here?"

The three looked around the grand room. No one was there.

"Don't you think that it was strange that there weren't any guards?" Aeneas said.

"This is the right room, isn't it?" Aramis asked.

"Yep, it is," Kat shrugged.

"So we just wait?" Aeneas asked Kat. Kat was preoccupied looking at the stately room.

The three waited and waited and waited for what seemed like an eternity. The room was sheer opulence. Marble floors covered in fine carpets. The bed was draped with floating silks canopied above it and over it. Gold jewelry splashed with jewels lay across side tables. Panels of red, green, and blue jewels were inset into the white marble walls.

"It's abit O.T.T don't you think?" Aramis said, picking up a necklace.

"Don't touch anything," Kat said to Aramis and Aeneas.

"I've never seen anything quite like this," Aeneas said, looking at all of the trunks that were studded with semi-precious jewels. "Such wealth. I've never seen such wealth before. She must truly be a grand wife. The king must love her to give her all of this. Even the water jug is silver."

Aramis sprawled himself out on the bed "Woah! Kat, this is the best bed I've ever felt". He lay his head back feeling like he was being eaten up by a cloud.

"I told you not to touch anything" snapped Kat, panic creeping up on her.

"Oh shush," Aramis said "We've waited for ever. What is the harm in having some fun while we are here?"

CHAPTER TWENTY-SEVEN

Finally, they heard footsteps coming towards the room. Aramis scurried off the bed. Kat, thinking fast, pulled both him and Aeneas into a hidden corner.

"Leave me," a voice commanded as the door opened and the three peered out to see if the princess was alone.

The princess seemed to float into the room on a cloud of billowing crimson silk draped over her body and her head. As she walked, small bells around her ankles gently rang.

She sat at a table looking into a finely carved marble mirror that was inlaid with blue flowers made of turquoise. Out of the corner of her eye, she caught a glimpse of something. She looked up to see the three standing in front of her. Startled, she knocked over a platter of fruit that crashed to the marble floor, making an almighty sound.

"I'm all right," she yelled to the guards outside her door. "I just dropped a platter. Stay where you are."

"Who are you?" she commanded. "Why are you in my room?"

The princess was tiny, even smaller than Kat. She was dressed in all of her finery, dripping head to toe in gold and jewels. Her tiny face peered from beneath the silk veil that covered her head. She had a small gold disc encrusted with jewels with a large emerald hanging at the end like a big green teardrop sitting in the middle of her forehead.

Aramis thought that they had the wrong room. She looked like a small doll.

"Why are you looking at me like that boy?" she hissed.

Oh no, not the B word, Kat thought.

"How old are you?" Aramis asked. "You look like you're, I don't know, nine or ten?"

"Thank you for that uneducated assumption," she quipped. "I'm thirteen, and how dare you presume anything about me." She directed her condescending, unimpressed tone to Aramis who was standing beside Kat, rolling his eyes.

"Great, we've got another nutter," he said.

"I'm Kat. This is my brother Aramis, and this is our friend, Aeneas and—"

"Yes, yes, I know why you're here," she said, waving her hand at Kat as if dismissing her. "I was told that you were to be here this morning. Well, I suppose you're here now, thank goodness. There was no way in hell I was marrying that fat old man tomorrow."

"You know why we're here?" Kat asked, looking puzzled.

"Of course I do. You, boy, come," the princess snapped her fingers at Aramis who stood looking around unaware that she was speaking to him. "I said *boy, come!*"

"Boy? Did you just call me boy?" Aramis said in a very disapproving tone. His face was so twisted that even Kat had to look at her twin brother twice. He stood beside Kat and Aeneas with his hands on his hips glaring straight at her.

"I am sorry, I was led to believe that there would be one among you that would be of masculine in body? If that is not you, then I apologize. Perhaps they were referring to ... ahem ... you," the princess sarcastically said, pointing at Aeneas.

"Come to think of it, you do look more feminine than masculine. Please accept my humblest apologies," she said sarcastically, smiling at Aramis.

"Katttttttttt!" Aramis shrieked, turning to his sister. "You better keep her away from me."

"Whaattttt? What did I do?" the princess smirked.

"Let's just go with the flow until we get what we need," Kat replied.

"And what would that be? Would it be this?" The princess was holding a crystal in front of the three. "You see wherever this crystal goes, I go. If I don't go, then no crystal, understand?"

"Perfectly," Kat replied.

"Great. You will address me as your majesty or Princess Gaia. Now, boy, fetch my things," Gaia snapped her fingers again to Aramis, smiling.

"Aramis … just take deep breaths, deep breaths," Kat said, holding him back.

Gaia was even starting to get on Aeneas's nerves.

"I can tell that you and I are going to be great friends," Gaia smirked, mocking Aramis. "What's wrong? Are you missing suckling your mummy, little boy?"

"Whoa! That's a bit uncalled for, isn't it?" Aeneas gasped.

"I'm sorry, boy, girl, whatever you are. I would say the same to you if I thought you even knew who your mummy was. I, on the other hand, am Princess Gaia, daughter of the Empress of Athens," she announced to the three as if addressing a royal court.

"Well, we've had quite enough from you, Gaia," Kat said, her face bright red and getting redder by the minute.

"That's Princess Gaia actually and your face is, ahem, as red as a … as a … hmmmm where have I seen a face as red as yours before? Thinking, thinking—oh yes, as red as a baboon's behind."

Aeneas gasped, not believing what she had just heard come out of the princess's mouth. Aeneas turned to Aramis, checking that he had heard what she had thought that she had heard, and from the look on his face, Aeneas could tell that he had.

"I think it's about to kick off," Aramis said, standing well back as the two small girls seemed to be preparing for an out and out war.

"As I said, *Gaia*, you better listen up. If you want to come with us, you had better lose that damn superior attitude that you have going on. There is no room for your rubbish! Do I make myself clear?" Kat was standing inches away from Gaia's face.

"Well, aren't we a stroppy one? Perfectly, perfectly clear. Now take off your crystals and put these on," Gaia said, handing them three blue crystals that looked exactly like theirs.

"I'm not taking mine off," Aeneas said.

"Neither am I," Aramis said.

"Nor I," said Kat.

"Fine, then go ahead and die here because, any second, guards will burst in and I will tell them that you are kidnapping me—your choice," Gaia snapped.

"Fine!" Kat snapped back.

"Fine," Gaia retorted.

"All of you put your crystals in those contraptions that boy has on his feet," Gaia said, pointing at Aramis's shoes.

"What's going on? How do you know about the crystals?" Kat asked Gaia.

"No time to explain. The guards should be here soon and we have to leave. This way. And you, boy, bring that bag. A princess never knows what she may need," Gaia said to Aramis.

Aramis was determined not to do as Gaia commanded and was about to walk past Gaia's bag, when Kat turned to him and mouthed, "Please, please take the bag."

Aramis rolled his eyes as he walked behind Gaia. He reached out his hands to pretend to strangle her.

"Tut-tut-tut, no strangling of the princess," she said with her head on its side as if she had eyes in the back of her head.

Aramis turned to Kat and asked, "Are we really taking her with us?"

"Afraid so," she replied.

"I can hear you. Now this way. The guards are out the front." The princess pushed a panel at the back of her room that led to a secret passage.

"Take this," she said to Kat, handing her a book that looked just like the BOP, "and put your one in my bag."

Kat's face said it all. "Why?" she asked, unwilling to part with the Book of Peace.

"Because I command you too," Gaia said, turning to challenge Kat. "Now, again put that book in my bag and take this one. We don't have much time," Gaia said, snatching Kat's satchel and rummaging through it for the BOP. "I'll explain everything later. But right now we need to get through this passage to the tunnels."

They took a step into the dimly lit passage. Aeneas looked uncertain. It was all happening rather fast and this wasn't the original plan. Aramis was still bickering with Gaia.

"Have you ever heard of 'please' or 'thank you'?" Aramis said, as he watched Gaia making the swap of the books.

"No, should I have? Are they servants? I don't trouble myself with the little people."

"Little people? Wow, you have such great people skills. You're gonna make a great queen and wife," Aramis replied, shaking his head.

"I intend to be neither, thank you very much."

"I'd say the king got off lightly," Aramis mumbled. He wondered how such poisonous words could escape from such a tiny little girl.

"Thank you, boy, and for your information, it is I who got off lightly. Do you know what it's like to be sold to the highest bidder like a common slave? No? Well, that's what my parents did. They sold me to that fat old sixty-five-year-old king for gold and jewels. I was a transaction. A business deal and I hope they rot in hell for doing that, selling their own daughter. Well, the joke's on them because when he finds out that I'm gone, he's gonna make them give all of that gold back!"

CHAPTER TWENTY-EIGHT

"We are nearing the tunnel and you need to do this now" the princess stated "Are you on board with me holding your book?"

Kat reluctantly agreed with the change as they met up with Devdash and his brothers.

"Quickly!" Davinder said. "This way please."

They all ran quietly out of the stone carved dark tunnels and down through the alleyway back to Suneel's house.

"Quick! In here," Suneel rasped.

As the three ran into the room, Vijaye grabbed Kat's bag.

"I'll be taking that, thank you," he jeered.

"What? My bag, why?" Kat asked.

"It's not the bag I need. It's this," he said, pulling out the (fake) BOP, throwing the bag back at Kat. Kat was astounded.

"But why?" Aeneas asked.

"Why? Well, come to mention it, hand over those crystals as well," Devdash said.

"Devdash, what's going on?" Kat asked.

"I'll tell you what's going on" The Princess spoke, "These are the Kumar brothers and are the infamous tomb-robbing brothers of India, famous for stealing anything that sparkles. You see these four are notorious for robbing all sorts of things—tombs, palaces. Anything that shines and glitters they take,"

"Hey, we're famous. She said famous," Vijaye said, laughing. The brothers were impressed to be known throughout all of India.

"Devdash, is that true?" Aeneas asked, looking disappointed that she had been tricked yet again.

"Well, look at it like this, and I think Aramis said it best. We are liberators, and we are liberating this book and your crystals," Devdash replied.

"So the story of your falling in love with a princess was a lie?" Kat asked Davinder.

"Of course it was. We heard the story of the star years ago. We met a man. He came to the fort and Suneel and him got talking," Vijaye said. "Actually, I was about to relieve him of some jewels that needed 'liberating' when he mentioned that very book and the crystals that lead to untold riches. He even told us when three visitors would arrive and what they needed to get. So my brothers and I hatched a plan that would make us rich. No more scrambling around in tunnels for us. And all we had to do was wait and then, just like we were told, a princess was offered to the king for his sixty-fifth birthday and then two days before his wedding the three visitors would arrive. We just had to wait for you to approach the fort and lead you in with our caravan. And everything has gone to plan." The brothers laughed. "It was so easy. Just as we were told it would be," they boasted.

"You deceived us, but I believed you. We believed you." Kat whispered

"And now for the best bit, before 'liberating the princess,' we had told the guards of your plan. That's why there were none at the fort. They're in on it too. They are on their way here now. You will be arrested for kidnapping the princess and will be, well, you'll obviously be killed and we will be the heroes that captured you and will receive a huge award, as well as this book and these crystals. The princess will be returned to be just another wife of that fat old king." The brothers laughed uncontrollably, slamming and bolting the door on the four.

Stunned by the betrayal, Aramis and Kat looked at each other.

"The whole thing was a setup? Seriously?" Aramis said, not fully comprehending everything that just unfolded.

"Seems that way. They seemed so nice, genuinely lovely," Kat replied.

Aeneas said, panicking. Panicking and pacing, "Oh no, oh no, oh no. We are going to die".

"No, Aeneas, remember we have the crystals and the right book, remember? We do have the right book, don't we?" Aramis asked Kat while bending down to take out the crystals out of his shoes.

"Yep, sure do." She turned to Gaia "But I don't understand. How did you know that this was going to happen?" Kat asked Gaia.

"I was visited in my homeland before making the journey here. A lady told me that three days before my intended wedding a caravan would come carrying the crystal. She told me exactly where in the caravan it was and then she told me that you three would arrive, and to do what I did."

"Who was she?"

"I don't know. Her name sounded like a flower. I can't remember, but she knew all about me and my life and that I did not want to marry that disgusting pig. She gave me a way out, so I listened."

They could hear the brothers celebrating outside the door, congratulating themselves on a job well done. Their wives were talking about all of the fine jewels that they would own and how gullible the four were.

"Let's get out of here before the guards arrive," Aramis said. "Gaia, I need your crystal, please," Kat said, opening up the BOP.

"Ready to go?" Aeneas asked Gaia, "It can feel a bit funny the first time, but apparently you get used to it"

"Wait, I have one more thing to do," Gaia said. She pulled out a note from her pocket.

The note read:

My dearest husband-to-be,

As I write this, I am consumed with fear. I fear for my life. I have been stolen from your home, my dearest. The four Kumar brothers Devdash, Davinder, Suneel, and Vijaye have promised to release me for a ransom, but I fear that they have sold me. I heard them saying that they could get twice the amount for me.

If you ever receive this note, know that I will always love you and the life that we should have had together. Revenge my death, my love.

Forever yours, Gaia

"Did you pre-write that?" Aramis asked.

"Of course I did," Gaia hissed, leaving the note under the carpet on the floor with the corner sticking out.

"The guards will come here, think that the brothers had tricked them, find the note, and the rest is history."

"Wow, you really are cold-hearted," Aramis said, watching Gaia putting her earring, a gift from the king, with the note.

"It's called survival, boy, survival!" she replied while making sure that you could just see the corner of the note.

"Cool story, mate. Now move it," Aramis muttered, pushing Gaia to move faster.

"You will regret that, boy."

They started to walk into the tunnel. Gaia paused and turned. "We really are going somewhere else, aren't we?" she asked.

"Yep, you all good to go?" Aramis asked.

"Yes, yes, I am," and with that she turned confidently and started to walk into the tunnel whispering to herself, "No regrets, no regrets, no regrets."

"Good," Aramis said, dumping her bag.

"Ummm, excuse me, I need that," Gaia said, pointing at her bag.

"Really? Hold on ... Do I have anything written here?" Aramis asked, pointing to his forehead, walking past her.

"No, no, you don't," Gaia replied puzzled.

"No? So I don't have Gaia's slave written on my forehead, no? Then carry your own damn bags. You have hands."

Gaia could hear Aeneas and Kat giggling.

"But ... but I'm a princess," Gaia said, stomping her feet.

"Not where we're going!" he laughed. He moved to stand beside Kat with a smile on his face, ready for the next adventure. "Where are we going, Kat?" he asked.

"Ireland and the map showed a ship." They walked into the tunnel.

"A ship? I don't do ships," Aeneas replied, walking into the tunnel of flashing lights and swirling stars.

Gaia screamed while stomping her foot on the ground again.

"Can someone carry my bag? I'm a princccceeeeeeesssssssss!"

EPILOGUE

SPAIN

"Ewwwwwwww, gross, princess puke on my runners," Aramis said, looking down at his shoes that Gaia had just vomited all over.

Gaia was sitting on the ground. She felt like her head was about to explode.

"Well, that time was easier," Aeneas announced proudly standing upright.

"Where exactly are we, Kat? This doesn't look like Ireland and it doesn't look like a ship," Aramis asked.

It was so hot. The air so dry. Definitely not Ireland. A huge mountain range stood in the distance. Kat reached into her bag to pull out the Book of Peace. "Can I borrow your crystal, please?" Kat asked Gaia who was busy throwing up.

Stepping through the growing puddles of vomit, Aeneas retrieved the crystal and handed it to Kat. Kat held it above the book, and they watched as the location of the next piece of the star came into view.

"Yeah, nah, definitely not Ireland. We're in Spain, which would explain the excruciating heat" Kat said as a 3D view of what looked like at least thirty horse-drawn carriages slowly meandered toward the four.

"Gypsies," Aramis said, watching the wagons traveling in the book. "This will be fun for the precious princess. She'll die of fright," he said, looking over to Gaia. "You may wanna get up and make yourself presentable, Princess? It's time to get to work," he yelled out to her.

The hot, dry, dusty road bounced every ray of sunlight up at the four as if they were being relentlessly stabbed with piercing hot spears. Every minute they waited seemed like a torturing hour. There were no trees or shade, and the four patiently waited for the wagons beside the side of the road.

The wagons grew nearer, and Kat took one last look at the book. She had a strange feeling and so did Aramis. Why did the book show Ireland and then send them to Spain? They looked at each other, both knowing that somehow this time would be different. It was an uneasy feeling. Kat couldn't quite put her finger on it.

The first wagon came into sight being pulled by the most magnificent horse any of the four had ever seen. It was decorated in sparkling jewels that became blinding in the unbearable sunlight.

Thankfully, the beautiful horse and wagon stopped. A weathered man wearing a straw hat looked down from the wagon at them, and then a woman looked out from inside the wagon. Her deep red wavy hair was covered by a yellow head scarf as her big hazel eyes peered at the four.

Aramis looked up at the woman in the wagon, and in complete disbelief, he gasped, "Oh my god, it's Lu!"

www.ingramcontent.com/pod-product-compliance
Lightning Source LLC
Chambersburg PA
CBHW070405200726
48294CB00003B/1089